The Work

The WORK

JD Hollingsworth

CASA FORTE PRESS

For information contact:

Casa Forte Press

Calle Gutiérrez Los Rios 47

14002 Córdoba, Spain

www.casafortepress.com

Book and cover design and illustrations by the author

ISBN: 978-8-40906-594-3

Printed in the United States of America.

First Edition: November 2018

10 9 8 7 6 5 4 3 2 1

CASA FORTE
PRESS

Vic
/
John

God lends a helping hand to the man who tries hard.

\- Aeschylus

The Work

Part 1

JD Hollingsworth

The Work

"That rain?"

"Them's yer las' words?"

"How's that?"

"A-comin'... uh huh, sounds like... But, that's all ya gots ta say on th' matter?"

"Ya mean f'I can do that?"

"Yeah... How I likes a ones with th' *co*-bras a-bitin' at th' mongeeses. Make 'im do that?"

"Well, I ain't *got* any *co*-bras, an' armadillos don't fight 'em even f'I did, ya know?"

"Hell, I know *that*, Anse. I jus' wan'it, okay?"

"'Bout a rattlesnake?"

"Dang... Everbody's got a rat'ler... Make it *look* like a *co*-bra?"

"Well, Mullis, how much money ya got?"

"Ahhh... Hellfire... aw'right, jus' put 'im on a log or sum'in'?"

"Didn't useta see 'em 'round here sa'much, all squashed in th' road an' everwhere an' all like now... Down closer't Florida, but not sa'much 'round here, 'member?"

"Uh huh. Troublemakers..."

Now, in nearly twenty years of business this was the first time a nine-banded armadillo had burrowed its way into Ansel Bragg's world. He had seen them, of course. His own mother had an armadillo handbag presented by her Aunt Ada when repatriated to Utinahica from out in Texas City after that fertilizer blast took out half the place in '47. This had lain, patient and forgotten, until young Ansel's Howard Carter-like search for the gifts of an approaching Christmas had lead to its discovery, entombed in the back of a cluttered closet nearabout two decades on. For the lad, this imbricated mummy emerged as the greatest gift of all. The hours spent exploiting that clutch

The Work

as football, weapon and confidant had, years on, lead the teenage Ansel to draw a bead upon a randomly passing animal with his .22, hoping to extract knowledge of what made fat the interior of one not rattling with a compact, tiny package of tissues and pair of white dress gloves. Poor eyesight and an errant shot might have prevented the travesty of that spontaneous and ham-handed novice vivisection that day. But things are what they are, if not always what they appear to be, and as it would come to pass, and in the end, these seemingly meaningless boyhood hours – as all seem, at the time, to be – had already determined his destiny, even if he himself would never know how, nor even realize it at all.

•••

A reasonably fit man of forty within, Ansel outwardly wore the more ill-fitting skin of one a few races nearer the glue factory: sagging here; pulling at the seams a bit there; glassy-eyed with fatigue. His was not a fatigue wrung from exertion, or external concern but, rather, emanated from a deep and ineludible insecurity. Still, with the crucial encouragement of his better half, he had made something of himself as owner of the Hide n' Skeet Taxidermy and Gun Range in Utinahica, deep in that flat, endlessly piney part of Georgia where nothing happens.

The shooting range was, to be truthful, nothing more than a field of fence post targets along a red dirt berm behind Ansel's maroon board-and-batten workshop and home at the edge of those piney woods out on Sapps Ferry, just down from the County Road. And – more truth be told – as Man annually extirpated the dove from Nature in greater numbers than any other beast in the state, there was no need to sacrifice those of clay, and, so, not a man in Torcall County actually shot skeet. Ansel just liked the name when his wife and backbone, Hazel, dreamed it up.

So, from one thing to another, followed a life wrapped up in skins. A life filled, and a life tied up, with the resurrection of the life-*less* to an eternal and glorious, if somewhat limited, new one. At least that's how Ansel saw it. But, be that as it may, other than Ada's old rolled poke and the victim of his youth, Ansel had never put his hands on a *Dasypus novemcinctus* in any meaningful way until Mullis Alewine presented the thing for him to prod, probe, and puncture with exploratory cuts from which to divine its taxidermic complications.

He had, then, thought the work to be as much a nuisance as the living things themselves had become of late and, so, put it away where it had now sat almost eight months in his

The Work

freezer. But considering it presently in the humdrum of his day-to-day, he sensed – foresaw – that the work could bring change to his predictable, ordinary life, and, as it turned out, even now, twenty years on, there are, among those who witnessed it, they who still swear the work he made of this one peculiar creature – and the change it did bring – was, if nothing else, the peculiarist thing they ever did see.

•••

I

A nsel required a form.

He tapped the hairpiece taped atop his thinning pate and pondered: armadillos were certainly known and so a taxidermy form would just as certainly be found among the catalogs he saw yearning for the floor in a precarious

The Work

heap atop the filing cabinet in which filing was a stranger: Van Dyke's, Trufitt, Skin City; One would provide – but at a decent time. It was too late.

"Tomorrow might be better," he thought.

Ansel, who his entire life had dressed exactly as had his own grandfather, molted the khaki pant and blue work shirt outfit that was, as much as any leopard's spots, his unchanging pelt, to cocoon himself in the equally unchanging flannels, worn abed in modesty each evening: even on the hottest August night, such as this. Being careful not to wake Hazel, he carefully pinned his peruke to a Styrofoam mannikin on his dresser, then stood in the darkness stroking it like a villain's cat as he became lost in thought.

These reveries were something for which Ansel had always been known. Indeed, his tendency to dream, to fantasize, to become so deeply lost within nested worlds of imagination, as to seem catatonic, had led to his schoolroom taunt – and eventually for any child not paying attention – as being "Ansleep." These flights of fancy were due, in part, to a true natural curiosity and inspiration, but also to need for a safe haven from the real world in which, until Hazel had come along, he had felt timid, nervous, and uncomfortable in his own skin. But now he allowed his mind to travel to a new and distant place of real wonder he was yet to understand as he stood gazing through and beyond the bedroom wall while smoothing the fur of his own head, down there on the vanity by his slightly overstuffed, middle-age paunch.

Hazel's suddenly renewed snoring hooked and reeled his astral envisaging back to their chamber, where time for true dreaming by her side, he thought, had arrived. But Ansel sat at the edge of the bed, staring at his corduroy slippers and debating their removal. Then, still in a state of fantastical wanderlust, he decided that before retiring he would allow the night to surrender just a few more moments of sleep to a quick flip through his collection of big wildlife picture books. He tiptoed to his office to pull out his *National Geographic* photo books, his *Sierra Club Wilderness Library* (which was as close as he would ever allow himself to get to the Sierra Club) and Attenborough's *Trials of Life*.

He flipped through the big glossy plates. As the zoetrope of predators: big cats, wolves, scorpions – and prey: wildebeests, antelopes, other scorpions – wheeled by, he ruminated upon Mullis' fancy, and there was a brilliant flash in his mind, and, he would later swear, a tap upon his shoulder: this could be... *different*. The never-ending battle, not just of beast against beast, but of foes as *forces* in opposition, metaphorical

The Work

eternal forces engaged in conflict for centuries, for millennia, for all of the years that ever were – of which Ansel knew there to be six thousand – could be portrayed through the proverbial rivalry of mamba and mongoose: The *Tyrannosaurus Rex* to the other's *Triceratops*, the Blofeld to its Bond, the Moriarty to...

Of course, as he had pointed out to Mullis Alewine, he didn't *have* any cobras. But he would worry about that later. He would make this work. "This *is*, after all, a metaphor..."

The possibilities energized him. In this near-sighted, scavenging ironclad, Ansel had found a new and unusual subject, inspiring a new and unusual approach. Something to which he could truly apply his skill. Not another fat bass on a board or cross-eyed bobcat on a Styrofoam rock, but something dynamic and compelling. Then, letting himself go to a place even Hazel could not provoke him to enter, he thought, maybe, possibly, he did not have just *skill*: an edge only honed on a blade picked up somewhere along the way. Maybe he had *talent*: an endowment hammered and folded in the forge of his own soul and ground on the wheel of his mind. Maybe even museum quality talent – like that of Perrygo, Pray, and Clark or – dare he think it? – Akeley...

He dug out a videotape of *Enter the Dragon* for more

inspiration. Was there anything that embodied battle-ready, zero-percent body fat animalism better than Bruce Lee? *He* would have been something to stuff.

Unable to restrain his inspired investigation he made his virgin attempt at a search of the Internet with this new "dial-up" thing. After enduring some unbearable screeching, like that of enraged fowl and the scraping of claws on a chalkboard, he found the search page and busied his mind on its use.

"Ask Alta Vista a question..." the screen beseeched: he thought not unlike the fortune-telling machines on the tables at Strickland's.

Question... question. What is the *question*?

"...Or enter a few words..." it went on.

This was better. His mind going in all directions, he entered wrestlers of the WCW: Lex Luger, Macho Man, Goldberg... Then "Holyfield," "Tyson." Then "animals, predators," "animals, predators, fighting," "animals, predators, fighting, death..." Then, in the small hours, he considered the Alta Vista results and stopped. He paused, and thought: There was *something more* he could add to the lengthening train of keywords. He raised his forearm, aimed his forefinger, and pecked "a" – "r" – "t."

The Work

The blue list slowly unrolled and, scrolling down, something caught Ansel's eye:

"Panther Surprising a Civet Cat."

Ansel clicked the cobalt enigma and an image, working down, pass-by-pass, slowly began to reveal itself on the screen. A patinated bronze emerged as the lines interlaced to freeze him where he sat. The artfully composed, dynamic and desperate, death and struggle-filled Nature of Antoine Louis Barye made him swoon.

And there were more:

"Bear Attacking a Bull."

"Elephant Crushing a Tiger."

"Ten-Point Stag Brought Down by Two Scotch Hounds."

"This, this is how I should have been doing it all along," he thought, his head spinning. "How we *all* should have." His mind reeled at this violence of the Wild; this pure eat-or-be-eaten conflict of Creation beyond Man's tempering Civilization in all of its stark, desperate, Bruce Lee, lean and muscular beauty.

"Stag Attacked by Lynx,"

"Bear Attacked by Dogs,"

"Wolf Holding a Stag by the Throat,"

"Python Killing a Gnu."

Each gushing with life.

Most importantly though, with that last one and with those to follow:

"Boa Eating a Gazelle,"

"Lion Crushing a Serpent,"

"Tigre dévorant un gavial,"

whatever that meant (but he could see it was a swamp cat beating up an alligator) – was mammals against reptiles: The good, loving and *be*loved, warm-blooded apex of Creation combating the evil, despised, cold-blooded bringer of Sin.

He was overcome.

His mind could barely contain it all.

He had to sleep before the birds began to sing ahead of the new dawn.

•••

The Work

II

Ansel did awaken to a new world late that morning. He pulled the armadillo out of the cooler and contemplated the frozen lump. He rolled it over in his mind, reshaping it; reimagining it; redefining it. His thoughts became filled with visions of armadillos: armadillos posing like body builders; armadillos bobbing and weaving like boxers; armadillos tapping like Astaire and waving by like Busby Berkeley chorus line. He had never felt so inspired. In fact, as far as he could now remember, he had never actually been inspired at all. There was, it seemed, too much potential in Art for him to even comprehend. *This* was new. New new. Like being born again. Like being baptized all over.

There would, any day now, come archery season's first white-tailed deer in the door to behead and gibbet. But, despite the ethic burned with a soldering iron into the wooden plaque hanging from a wire above his work bench,

It's not the work you

get in,

It's the work you

GET OUT!

there would be, he reasoned, plenty of time for the routine, bill-paying work. Shoot, he could do *those* jobs in his sleep; this could not wait. So Ansel thought about what Mullis wanted. He puzzled over it through the night deep into fitful fever dreams of creativity and in daydreams at the wheel that had nearly taken him off the road. He imagined the French name for his masterpiece – "*Armadillo dévorant un Rattlesnakeo*"

16

The Work

– and wondered had these combatants known one another any less than those fanciful pairings he had seen in Barye.

"Form! *Dag...*" he called out loud when he broke from his latest mystical visions and vainglorious fantasies. "I still need..."

He had not yet secured the next essential component: a form, the electrode upon which his vision would anodize. He went to the pile of catalogs that had finally achieved the pine floorboards, flipped through a handful and thought he remembered seeing what he needed in... *this one.* Stalking his game through VanDyke's, he carefully peeled each page back to peer around its edge, occasionally pausing to observe other wildlife along the trail: Aardvark; African bongo; "Hey, there's that civet cat...huh, whudd'ya know..."

Spotting the quarry in his scope, he licked his pencil and itemized each trophy on the gridded ledger of the order form to bag them:

• 1/ Item # DLO-600, Lifesize Armadillo, Standing, Left Turn.

These forms are known for requiring little alterations.

"Check," and he laughed, knowing full-well that the pageant he envisioned would require far more than "little alterations."

• 1/ Item # MGO-600, Lifesize Mongoose, Standing, Right Foot Up, Right Turn.

"Check... What else, what else?"

He had plenty of Bondo and wire and

"... Ah!"

• 1/ Item # UFG10, Urethane Foam, Bipartite, 10 Gallon Kit

"I don' know... 10 gallons... That's a lotta chemical..." he thought, "but, it'll get used... 'Specially f'I get really fired up."

He called North Carolina, placed the rush order, then sat and stared through the phone on his workbench, absent-mindedly drumming his fingers and dreaming of what was, even now, already heading his way.

•••

The Work

III

In the here and now, Ansel knew that in the meantime there was plenty to do with the thawing little glyptodont. He put it in the microwave on defrost then gathered up his currier's knives, X-Actos, spoons and cabinet scrapers for defleshing. It was more difficult than he had hoped. The tiny, taloned burrowing feet, the thin, leathery head and snout, the stiff, rough hide were each a caution and working inside the hard, boat-like carapace was something between open-heart surgery and hollowing out a jack-o'-lantern. Ansel disposed of the bone, muscle and other tissue in a rusty fifty-five gallon drum along with the remains of various other beasts and the excess resins and solvents of his trade's processes. He would periodically haul this portable toxic waste site and charnel house out to the long-derelict remains of Hazel's family chicken farm and dump the slurry of volatile organics and animal matter into the pit with the large residual blob of funk that was once the scrapings of henhouse fecal pans. Other times Ansel would invite his few friends over for evening barbecues where the drum's contents would be set ablaze as they made for an excellent bonfire.

After removing the being from its shell, scraping the slippery inside of the hide clean and preparing the empty mantle for degreasing and tanning, he cleared away some space in the workshop for the custom work he planned for the mounts and beyond. Then, as when some unpleasant, unwanted memory descends to weigh down and rob a moment, a sadness overcame him. It was only just now, with this prehistoric roadkill before him, that he had become aware of the artist that had toiled away, frustrated, deep inside his own hide, yearning to rend asunder the sutures that bound *it*. This realization, and the new world it heralded, might have been uplifting, yet it had made him aware of the things he *could* have done: the dramatic frozen ballet of the wild he could have choreographed; the exotic and far-away zoological wonders, beyond the tiresome woodland pests of Georgia he had statically posed like department store dummies for decades, that he might have granted a worthy hereafter. The lost time, lost opportunities, for his soul's expression made him feel as if he himself had been filled with

The Work

sawdust since his first amateur opossum in 1968.

•••

FedEx arrived with bundles from Van Dyke's and Ansel could scarcely contain his ambition now that work on his magnum opus could begin. As he set to re-work the styrene form for the mongoose/armadillo amalgam, his own mind seemed to cede control of his actions and he began to work as if the agent of an outside force. Filled with that first night's revelations – the photos, the kung-fu films, the French table bronzes with their high-browed savagery – he began to work like an automatic writer, reshaping, combining and editing the two distinct forms, like a Frankenstein's monster, into one new, wholly other, thing. Arms reached and rotated, hands turned and filed, fingers twisted wire and skimmed Bondo to fill the voids and sculpt new and unknown muscle groups. All the while it seemed he was only a spectator to the artistry and workmanship occurring before him.

At last there it was, skinless and unfinished. Still, the beige polymer thing, blotched with salmon-hued patches of un-

JD Hollingsworth

sanded Bondo, was perfect.

He began to weep.

•••

The Work

IV

Early the next morning he had one more important task. He grabbed a burlap feedbag, an old iron garden rake, a can of gasoline and went out into the brush. Six hours later he returned with his bag stinking of fuel and dancing to the rhythm of maracas. He filled the slop sink with water and dropped the bag in, pushing it to the bottom with the rake and holding it there until the pulsating burlap became saturated. Ansel then dropped sundry metal things from around the shop to weigh it down: a couple of railroad spikes, a ball peen hammer, an old cowbell.

The sack rolled rhythmically – hypnotically – then kicked violently, then more, then less, then a little, then, and at last, not at all, and he smiled because it was good. He would let it rest until morning.

For most of the next week he worked in secret, even locking up the shop to labor on the work. He toiled late into the night, which led to sidelong glances and whispers in town about what he was up to. What he *was* up to was forcing the armadillo's skin and plated exoskeleton to follow the commands of the hybrid form he had fashioned. In the end it had fit mostly well. The inadvertent, twisted, somewhat pinched-on-one-side expression of its face had, he thought, given it a determined, pugnacious visage which he would claim, *ex post facto,* to have been his intent all along.

Aside from accommodations for the low-voltage wiring, the snake was far easier. After slitting its throat and folding the head back like a PEZ dispenser, Ansel peeled off its skin as if it were a gym sock, pausing only to cut away the connective tissue at the anal plate. After skinning the head, scraping, soaking the

The Work

skin in dish soap and tanning, he unrolled the prolapsed, glycerin smeared tube back over a baling wire, pipe hanger's strap, and silicone armature of his own making. He made the electrical connections to the metal forked tongue he had hammered out and soldered from fence wire. Then, after a few details and fills sculpted from Critter Clay, and only enough slow-setting hide paste to allow working time, he bent and posed it in a way that pleased him much.

It was the world in which it all would reside, though, that would really tell the story, that would elevate this beyond his previous, pedestrian, commercial work and probably beyond anything ever so much as dared. This most ambitious aspect of a most ambitious work required the use of a variety of materials never before attempted in taxidermic tableaux. He made trips to Home Depot, RadioShack, and the Plants n' Pretty's Nursery and Gift Shop up in McRae. He ordered components from Edmund Scientific and Carolina Biological Supply. He took two days off at a dove hunting plantation near Thomasville where he marveled at the open, soaring long leaf pine cathedrals of light and wildflowers like had once stretched from Texas to Virginia before agriculture and fire suppression replaced it all with the scrubby, tangled woods like those along Sapps Ferry. He stopped by Mullis' corn patch with his shotgun on the way back, causing his friend to wonder. Finally, and with conflicted conscience, he enlisted the assistance of his sister-in-law's swain, Robert, in acquiring certain required paraphernalia to which Bobby had easy, if questionable, access.

At last supplied with all essential materials and metaphors, Ansel set to work on what he felt in his bones would be his triumph. He hoped to finish in the few weeks he had before firearms season, when the deer walking in his red door must retake their rightful place in his life and his time with the work would come to an end. Then in a feat credited to the Holy Spirit, the work was completed, again in secret and through the night, by the following Sunday – less than a week, before October first's new moon – and yet precisely recreating what he had seen in his mind's eye while laying next to Hazel and staring at the ceiling fan spinning above them in their rented bed.

But it would have to wait for a proper unveiling to be seen in this world.

•••

The Work

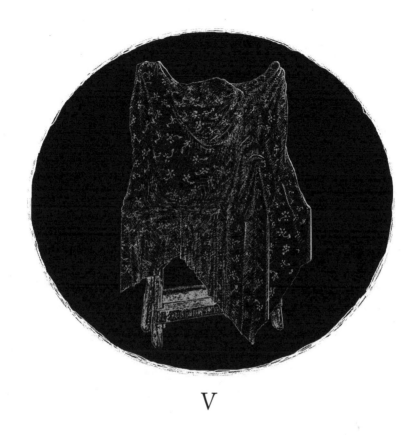

V

In spite of Ansel's urging and impatience, it was that Wednesday's new moon before Mullis Alewine could make it to the Hide n' Skeet to view the work – and even then it was he who seemed put out. Over the years Mullis had picked up, probably, twenty jobs from Ansel – deer, birds, fish – but he had never had to wait for a daisy-covered sheet to be pulled from them before he was allowed to even see them, much less take them home.

"Dang Anse, what th' Hell? Y'embar'sed 'bout it or sumpin'?" he griped.

"Hold on. I jus' want ya ta see it all't once."

"All't once? How else can ya see it? Part a it in a diff'rnt room?"

"Jus'… ahh, here… "

Ansel reached down at the front of the flowery linen heap to delicately pinch each corner, then quickly but carefully lift it over the top. He paused briefly to unsnag it from the metal signpost, then cleared the work and stepped back again, biting his lip and reflexively re-folding the sheet as he beheld his triumph.

Ansel's own reaction was as if he himself had never before viewed the work. The shock of the new caused him to catch his breath and wonder what he was seeing: seeing for the first time. A thing, in and of itself, an artistic, aesthetic marvel: but as its hidden, wondrous, message, the message – deep inside, but in some way known, like the unseen styrene that in there held the player's shapes – overtook the nerve impulses carrying that simple, superficial, beauty to his brain, he took a step back, dropping the folded sheet, and absent-mindedly touched his

The Work

hand to his heart.

The tear that welled in his eye did not blind him to the fact that awe was not his alone. Mullis Alewine likewise dropped his Days O' Work pouch and stood dumbfounded – staring and mute. Even not switched on it was the single most moving thing he had ever seen. And it had only cost him one hundred dollars.

Bragg agreed that that was a deal; surely worth far more in this world, particularly after beheld in full operation. Still, he felt it to be the product of a calling; something he had been commanded to create: he was only a tool in God's hand and doing the work of the Lord was its own reward. Or most of it: the Tesla coil alone had cost him almost the purchase price and, calling or not, he was running a business.

Having paid his hundred dollars Mullis had, on the one hand, wanted to take it home immediately but, upon reflection, felt that first it should be kept on display for some time at the Hide n' Skeet for all to see. Ansel's faith and therefore unwillingness to fall with pride had, at first, made him refuse for the sinfulness of that emotion. Mullis was adamant, though, would have it no other way and so, for the sake of the larger good, Ansel, at last, relented.

"Jesus H, Bragg... thing like this... gotta be seen. *Jus' gotta...*"

JD Hollingsworth

"I... I never realized somethin' like this... were even... in me... never seen this comin'," Ansel swooned with spiritual wonder. "The Lord does work in mysterious ways, Don' 'e?"

"I'll say," Mullis concurred. "Never hear the one what gets ya."

•••

30

The Work

VI

Over the coming days and weeks, word spread around town and from time-to-time a fair-sized group would be assembled in the shop. Sometimes five or six at once stood communing with the work – more than had ever before been in the place at one time, except during the March turkey shoots at the range. After the feature in the weekly *Utinahicayune*, people were in and out most every day and youngsters stopped by after school to gawk and teens to yell *"aw'right!"* People came from as far away as Fitzgerald, Hazlehurst, even from the onion capital, Vidalia. Then, when a small piece ran as "human-interest" filler on the Macon Fox News affiliate, it became a moderate regional sensation.

Requests to accommodate church groups, scout troops and Odd Fellows began coming in. There were inquiries into dates and places for local appearances and its touring schedule –

which, up until then, did not exist. There was even interest in publishing a review from *Breakthrough Magazine.*

"*Jee*-zoo," thought Ansel, "that's the gal darn *National Geographic* a the trade. *The Bible*... 'member when it was jus' up in Loganville... "

It was all becoming a little too much now for Ansel Bragg but, as Mullis opined: "Brother Bragg, this is bigger'n both a us."

•••

The Work

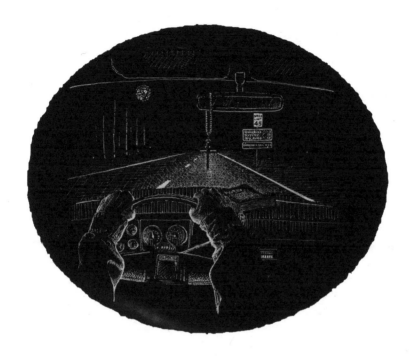

VII

F our months on, between the traveling and working to keep the bills paid and the doors open at the Hide n' Skeet, Ansel was exhausted. Mullis and he had even begun splitting tour duties. Mullis would not go out-of-state, though, so it was a road-weary Ansel Bragg that sat in a Waffle House across the lot from a Birmingham Rodeway Inn waiting for a cup of coffee to revive him for his evening call to Hazel.

The waitress brought him the steaming cup, pinching it by the handle and warning him "Careful, Honey, that cup is *hot – as – blazes!*" then flapped her hand wildly from the burn after dropping it down hard. Daydreaming about Springfield, Illinois and the World Taxidermy and Fish Carving Championships coming up there in just over a month, Ansel gripped around the entire barrel of the radiant cup, held it momentarily, then lifted it without reaction until the scalding liquid seared his tongue.

"*Hot* a'mighty!" he called out, sputtering, as the blistering coffee dribbled back out of his parboiled mouth – mostly back into the cup he still gripped fully in his hand, then placed gingerly back upon the counter.

"I *toad'ja* babe!" the waitress reprimanded, "I don' know how y'even picked that thang *up*."

"Dag!" He flicked his tongue in and out like a snake. "Ow…Durn tongue's burned numb now… I *hate* that."

Ansel tossed two dollars to the Formica and walked out, heading back to the room for his call. The waitress stepped over to swipe up the money and wipe up the drool. She picked up the nearly full cup then dropped it immediately, spilling most of it and yelling, "*Dammit!* Tha's *still* hotter'n…" As she sopped the

The Work

Jus' weird

molten brown puddle up into her rag she looked at her reddened fingers, then raised her eyes to watch Ansel, curiously, through the glass as he walked around the corner, still grimacing and flicking his tongue.

"Well... tha's jus' weird," she said to herself.

Ansel sat to make the call to his wife out of loneliness, but also to ask her to get an appointment with Dr. Pirkle about this exhaustion and stress and the dry skin it was causing. He also asked if she had seen the confirmation paperwork for the Championship. He was afraid it had been lost in one of his piles or even thrown out.

The positive semi-regional response and press he had already received had emboldened him to believe he could win a coveted Master Class, Best in World Award for the work and he planned to enter it in several sub-categories to increase his chances. Hazel said she had not seen anything, asked why he was "talkin' funny," and doubted anything had ever been thrown out since he started all of this anyway, but took the opportunity to point out, once again, that the entrance fees and hotel reservations had been a burden on the household, particularly with his not working as much of late, not to mention having to pay the Thompson boy, who had been apprenticed to work on

The Work

the basic shop and prep duties that needed to be done in Ansel's absence... and, by – the – way, Aaron Rents was calling and close to leaving them without a bed to sleep in.

He told her his tongue was burned and not to worry about all that because with the support he had been getting from the religious community, the Lord would certainly be looking after their well-being.

The current place of display was, in fact, in the Family Center of the impressive, two-thousand seat, Portal of Glory Baptist Church of Greater Birmingham, under the direction of the noted Rev. Dr. Raymond A. Bullock, Sr. who had himself described the work as,

> A work of the utmost artistry, whose inspired creation was most surely guided by the hand of the Holy Spirit as having captured in flesh and wadding the eternal battle between the unholy power of the serpent of sin and the righteousness of our Lord Jesus Christ as defended by his archangel warrior, Michael – the armadillo.

But, even as Ansel spoke those words of higher-calling

encouragement, he dreamed of the praise and adoration his peers among the laity would shower upon him in Springfield and the ticket to a better life it might provide. Albeit, his responsibilities with the work had left little time to work on even the routine bread-and-butter jobs coming in and practically none at all to move forward with his grand vision of a new and inspiring taxidermy. His efforts had, truthfully, not lived up to the promise of his first creation. The only other piece he had even attempted – a depiction of the Last Supper in squirrels and raccoons, with a fox as Judas – had seemed, even to him, obvious and weak. The lamb as Christ was well out-of-scale. He abandoned it three disciples in.

He had set the bar pretty high right out of the gate, though, so he chalked it up to sophomore slump.

Meanwhile the nervous exhaustion and stress he had complained of had also left him with numerous accidental cuts from careless slips of his tools. He had been so distracted and tired that he hadn't even felt them. Now, another week and a half through Montgomery, Phenix City, Americus and Cordele was a lot of driving: a lot of looking at his dry and flakey hands at the wheel. Maybe it was psoriasis. It did kind of look like his sister-in-law's elbows.

The Work

It was late when Ansel pulled in to the shop's gravel lot, but he didn't want to leave the work in the camper top overnight, so he rousted Hazel to help him push it off the tailgate and tote it into the shop.

She didn't say anything until, lugging one side of the work bowlegged across the gravel and almost to the open garage door, she declared, "Anse, I swear ta God... I know you love this thing but it's takin' over your life."

"Don't talk that way..." he demured. The way she had referred to the work as "this thing" had stung him. "It's not a 'thing.' "

"Well, what the heck is it then, Anse?"

"It is what it is..." he dissembled.

She dropped her end down a little too hard on the old door and sawhorse table and he knew that that tautology was not going to fly, but struggled to define what the work truly was – to him.

"It's somethin'... It's somethin's taking me places. Gonna take *us* places." There was longing in his voice.

"*Places?* What? Valdosta? Tallahassee? *Swains*-boro? Well, whoop-*dee*-doo. I better buy a new gown. Oh, wait! We'd need money for that."

"Aww... C'mon Haze." He started putting the sheet

back over it. "This's made me... I dunno... Important. Folks like it. Like me for it. And it's gonna... it's gonna lead ta somethin' I know. Somethin' big."

"Ohh, Anse..."

"Okay. Can we go to bed?"

"Yeah... You got a 'pointment Wensdee. Good Lord, get them hands looked at. Look like my sister's elbows."

•••

The Work

VIII

Tired? Well, I don't doubt it Anse, runnin' all over God's creation like ya do and workin' back here too. I believe that would tucker out a much younger man," Dr. Pirkle said pulling the tongue depressor out of Ansel's mouth.

"Only forty, Alvin." Ansel wiped his mouth on the back of his sleeve.

"Only forty-one next month, Anse, still, time does take its toll. But ya say this has only started since ya been doin' all this runnin' around?"

"Yeah. Past few weeks... month maybe."

"So," the doctor went on, lighting a cigarette "what is it, exactly, you'd like me to do?"

"I don't know... Fix it. Make it better. Some kinda... tonic or vitamins or... An' my hands are real dry and... Well, heck, *you're* the doctor..."

"Yes, I suppose I am and what *I* would prescribe is that ya slow down... Take it a little easier. Put some a your wife's face cream on 'em. Hands prob'ly just dried up from workin' with the things ya do."

"... I *do* use that caustic soda for bleachin' skulls. I guess that coulda made 'em... But, heck Alvin, I done used that for near thirty years... This's like... like back'en I started the Hide n' Skeet, back twen'y years on now and, 'member how I got all... weariful? From my nerves? Anyway, can't stop right now. I gotta keep on this for jus' a while longer. Jus' a while. So maybe ya can jus' give me somethin' for... I got bad nerves. I been sorta... losin' control a my tools a little, from the nerves I figure, and cuttin' myself an'... an' it's funny, I don' even really know it's happened till I see it. An' -" he pushed his sleeves up and reached out "maybe that's wha's makin' me have this sur-eye-sis..."

"Psoriasis? *Anse*..." The doctor took Ansel's hands and rolled them around squinting. "Well, these *do* appear to be cuts..." he mumbled. "Say you been getting 'em lately... from your taxidermy tools?"

"Yeah. It's like... like I can't hold my knives an' stuff right. Bad nerves... I reckon."

"Uh huh... And flakey. And ya say you don't feel it?"

42

The Work

"No."

"Even now? And when I squeeze 'em?" he said while pulling on the fingers like he was milking them.

"No. Not really. No."

Dr. Pirkle went to a drawer and put on some latex gloves. He came back and picked Ansel Bragg's hands up into the light and poked them and dragged the tips of his gloved fingers across the pale snakeskin-like patches on the backs.

"What is it Alvin?"

"Well Anse, I don't think this is psoriasis."

"Well, what is it?"

"So you work with all these dead animals... you work with anything unusual, prob'ly a while back. Some years or so back maybe?"

"Years? No. Same old stuff. What is it?"

"Hmmm... Well, I'm gonna make a cut here... get a sample..."

"Heck fire, Alvin. Ya can't jus' say somethin' like that an' not tell me what you're thinkin'. Is it cancer? *Skin cancer?* It's cancer."

"No. I don't know *what* it is. I'm just gonna send a sample out to the lab."

"*Lord.*"

"Don't go all end-times on me Anse. You feel that cut just now?"

"No..."

"Everbody gets things sent t'a the lab nowadays for everthing. You know that. Ever time ya spit in a jar or pee in a bottle, goes t'a lab. Prob'ly just dry skin, like you say. Nerves. Anyway, know in a week or so..."

"Aw'right Alvin... 'Doctor'... I'll be out on the road again jus' a few more days. Commitments. Back first a the week."

"Land's sake, you're like one a those rock and roll music stars, on the road the way you are... Anyway, remember... "

"I know," Ansel sighed, "*Drink water 'til ya pee water...*'"

"That's right. Live forever. So long Anse."

"So long."

"Oh, Anse..."

"Yeah?"

"Don't go a-puttin' your hands in Hazel's face cream... after all."

When Ansel got back to his workshop he looked over how the apprenticed Thompson boy's work was going, mumbled, "I gotta have a talk with that boy..." then went to

The Work

building a wooden crate to protect the work. There had been too many close calls with damaging it with all the travels and loading. He really didn't want to lose those asphalt corners. It was essential they remain sharp… and those birds…

He measured the truck gate and the camper top and figured that, even with the signpost, it would just clear the open camper door with the new crate, which relieved him some. He was still worried about what Dr. Pirkle had told him. Or, more accurately, what he had not.

Hazel came in from the house, sat on the edge of the workbench and looked around the room while Ansel tinkered with his boards.

"Wha's goin' on there, Haze?" he said without looking up.

"Oh, nothin'. Just got off the phone with m' sister."

"Norma?"

"Mm hmm."

"Ever'thing okay?"

"Naw. Robert again. Fightin'…" she sighed. "I don't know. I swear, I don't think Bobby's ever talked ta her once what wasn't all words with sharp edges and corners… "

"He's a… rough country fella," Ansel said as he stopped to look up and stare through the wall. "Whole family. I don' know how she ever got hooked up with that whole Rangle's Branch bunch anyways. Ever one of 'em's been on the road gang."

"Well she's lived a diff'ernt kinda life than us and made a pretty obvious bad choice."

"'Bout as bad as you can make…'round here. Maybe not in the city, but 'round here. An' cuttin' words ain't the half a it. How many times you seen her with a shiner?"

"Well I'd like ta nail *his* hide ta the wall but, Lord, I ain't gonna start runnin' down m'own flesh and blood for makin' a mess a her own life, but Anse… you come home, didn't say *nothin'* 'bout what happened at Dr. Pirkle's"

"He… well, he kinda didn't say nothin'."

"How can a doctor not say *nothin'*, Anse?"

"He… took some skin cuttin'," he held up his bandaged finger then put it back down, "an' sent it off ta some lab somewheres for some test or somethin'."

"*No!* Lord babe! What's that mean? Is it cancer? *It's cancer*. Is it cancer?"

"No. No, it ain't cancer. But I couldn't make hide nor hair a what he *was* a-sayin'. Talkin' what I done years ago and tests and pullin' on my fingers like a cow's tit – "

"*Anse!*"

The Work

" – an' talkin' 'bout your face cream…"

"My *face cream?* Lord, what in… I feel like the whole durn world's just gone nutty today. Just send everybody up ta Milledgeville… But he didn't think it was nothin' serious?"

"No."

"You ain't lyin' ta me?"

"No. An' anyways know next week," he reassured.

"Lord, Lord… Well, Lord… Anyway, Norma wants ta get outta the house and we need some things for the camp so we're gonna ride over't the Big Lots over Tifton."

"That's a good ride. Ya know I'm goin' on the road tomorrow an' I could use a ice chest. Cut down on cost a grub… Long as you're there."

"On the road, on the road…"

"Jus' a few days, Haze. Really. Up ta Perry for the 4-H, down ta Radium Springs Church over at Albany, stop by Omega the way home…"

"*Omeeega?* What's in that *po*-dunk end-a-the-road town?"

"School assembly, Monday lunchtime. Be out early, home for supper."

"Alright… fffffffffsshhhh… Getcha stirefoam chest. Okay, I'm goin' in, wait for Norma… grab a *Co*'cola. You want 'nything?"

"No."

"Okay, I'll see ya."

"Haze?"

"Yeah"

"Love you."

"Love you too, Anse."

She knew he did, but he rarely said it.

It worried her.

•••

The Work

somethin's

IX

I t was two-hours up to Perry. The Georgia Junior National Livestock Show was a big event running from Thursday to Sunday, but Ansel just wanted to do Friday. Friday evenings are the best and the exhibit halls would be filled with visitors from around the state and beyond. And with his temporary health issues and another long drive down to Albany for the Sunday presentation at Radium Springs, he was trying to budget his time and keep his exertion and stress level low.

It rained on and off the whole way, but the lead gray skies and rhythm of the wipers calmed him somehow and took his mind off his worries. Besides, this would be a good night. He could feel it. He liked fairs with their distracting clamor and hubbub that allowed him to, in his own meek way, let his hair down, yet rennin unseen.

He arrived at the Georgia National Fairgrounds and Agricenter around noon and parked in front of the big metal "Heritage Hall." A young Future Farmer of America wandering by during a break in the rain saw Ansel struggling to pull the wooden box from the camper to the tailgate and offered help. He retrieved a dolly from the big red Butler building, helped drop the work on the cart and roll it to Ansel's booth, right up in the center aisle: another good sign.

When he learned what it was that he had transported, the fresh-faced kid with the respectable haircut and FFA sweatshirt was excited to have been right there to help.

The Work

"I heard about this, sir. Read about it in the paper. *The Telegraph*! I was hopin' to see it, but now I got to help bring it in! Wait 'til I tell 'em back at school!"

"Well, son... what's your name?"

"Roy Wayne. Roy Wayne Byce."

"Well, Mr. Roy Wayne Byce, you help me pull this box here off a the top an' you'll be the very first ta see it... here."

"Yes sir!"

The box had barely cleared the first crow when Roy Wayne Byce let out, "Ho-ly...!"

Ansel said, groaning, "Aw'right... Let's set this box down outside the booth an'... I can take it right out ta the truck after I get this all set up an' whatnot... Uhhh, Oh my... Okay... huh There. (sigh) Wooo."

Again, the boy proclaimed, "Ho-ly. I swear ta... I ain't never seen... nothin'..."

A big woman dressed like a forest ranger in a khaki shirt and shorts was putting out brochures at the booth across the aisle. She saw what was going on and strolled over.

"Well, that's... int'resting."

"Sure is!" Roy Wayne interjected.

"Thank you. Thank ya much." Ansel said, glowing.

"Is this a... part of a... a highway safety display?"

"No ma'am. No it's… well, it's sort of a work of Faith. An' Hope."

"I see. Okay…" the forest ranger woman said, curiously. "I was just wondering… with the road sign and all. What else will you have?"

"This is it. The whole shee-bang," Ansel chuckled.

"In'tresting. Well, I hope the message gets through."

"Yes ma'am. I believe it will. I like ta think. 'Ventually it's gonna have to sink in. Draws some kinda crowd anyways."

Roy Wayne pointed out with regret that he had to get back to his potential prize hog across the way at Sheep/Swine Barn #1 but hoped to stop by again later. After he had helped roll the crate back and slide it into the truck Ansel opened a cardboard box, grabbed a handful of the brochures he had gone all the way to Albany to print at Kinko's and asked Roy Wayne to pass them around if he would.

"*Yes sir!* I sure will!"

Ansel walked back in thinking what a good boy that was, and knew that with all the 4-H-ers and real Bible-believing farm kids like him around that tonight would be a real good "show." Real good.

He walked over to the booth across from his, as the forest ranger woman was about to take off until later in the

The Work

afternoon. He asked if she'd like a brochure, which she accepted. She stood looking it over, flipping it from one side to the other, and saying "In'tresting, very in'tresting." Her hair, knotted into a tight bun at the back of her head, pulled the skin of her big round face to give it the squinting look of a suspicious – or perhaps, watchful – person, but also into a permanent, knowing smile, like a dolphin. Ansel noticed things involving skin and its properties, but was also aware of what lay underneath. She had an air of intelligent inquiry and a powerful serenity that made him feel secure and that she was actually paying attention: seeing, knowing, aware. He liked her and hoped she would notice the outline drawing of the work with the number key and legend to what it all meant, of which he was justly proud. He thought it made it real professional looking, like the didactic panels on the nature dioramas at the museum up at the state capitol.

Ansel noticed the "Georgia – la Roquefort" embroidered on her shirt and printed on the big photograph behind her of a forest in perfect lines, like a Magritte painting.

"You inta lumber products?" he asked.

"Hmmm?" she said looking up from the guide. "Oh... Well, in a way. I'm here from the seed orchard up in Putnam County, up on the lake up there."

"Seed orchard. Huh... I never... Guess I never thought about it."

"Seeds. Yes sir. Gotta have seeds. Everything's gotta have a seed." She began her exhibition presentation. "So we have an orchard of what we call 'supertrees' from which we harvest the cones, extract the seeds in a kiln – see, these trees are programmed by nature to have their cones open up by the heat of the forest fires as they pass through and when they can drop their seeds to the cleared earth and take root. So we heat 'em up – the cones – in a kiln, then collect the seeds that fall out and plant them so we can always depend on having top-notch, disease-resistant, fast-growing and superior-yielding... you would call them 'forests,' but we call them 'crops.' Sustainably planted, harvested and replanted around the South year-after-year."

"Well, I'll be..."

He took one of her brochures, went back to tidy up his own booth and as he did thought to himself "In'trestin.' A seed. That's right. Everthin's got ta have a seed. With a seed, a good seed, a strong seed, spilled on the ground, great things'll grow an' spread... Ground jus' needs ta be cleared, made ready – by the fire a His Word, by the terrible times at hand – for my message."

The Work

•••

Perhaps it was the intermittent rain, but the evening was not yet as busy as Ansel had hoped. Still, it was early and he felt okay about leaving his booth, now and then, to wander – though always staying within sight of the work. To the left of his booth was the big Richard, with the close-cropped beard carved to make him look like he had a chin. He was with the Middle Georgia Black Powder, Archery, Truncheon and Primitive Weapons League, or the MGBPATaPWL – which Richard said as a word and which Ansel heard as "the incompatible." He had a collection of bows, old flintlock rifles, powder horns and such. He and his fellow MGBPATaPWL members – primitive weapons hunters with their own set of state regulations and hunting seasons – were, he said, purists: "Downright Luddite."

"Tag says 'Richard,' call me Dick..." he said, puffing himself up. "Yeah, state regulations say black powder muzzleloaders, bows, crossbows... Which is *all* fine an' dandy. 'Cept, funny though, they'll consider a break action, in-line muzzleloader with a 12x20x62 Zeiss scope with range-finding reticles, speed loaders, pellet powder, *and saboted and jacketed bullets* to be a 'primitive' weapon. Ha! Right! Ya know what I'm saying?" (He did not.) "Oughta be flintlocks, bows, atlatls... An' don't get me started on compound bows. Like I said, that's fine. No problem with a CB, but you're talking 'primitive'... Talk to the hand, man. Primitive: *Not*! An' man, I tell you what, when the shit hits the fan – an' *it will* – you *do-not* want to *not* be able to defend your clan or feed your children because *the wheel* on your bow broke? Am I right, bro? That's a GD joke son. Hell, I knap my own points."

Ansel thought Richard was very intense and his energy made him a little nervous. All he really knew about the displays in Richard's booth was that the stuffed black bear and turkey were, at this time, a month after and a month before their respective seasons. It's just the kind of factoid he was aware of from years of watching the work come in season-after-season.

Ansel examined the taxidermy work on the bear as he walked back. There was a little sign hanging from a wire around its neck: "Somethin's Bruin." There was. Things seemed... not right with the world somehow. There was a lot of change: crazy change and worry. He knew it, the bear knew it, Richard there talking about when the... when "it," was going to hit the fan, knew it. Something was brewing all right. This was the reason

The Work

for his having been called.

Why he was being called now.

"… Mr. Bragg! Mis-ter Bragg!"

"What… " Ansel came out of his reverie staring the bear in the face. "What… What!?"

He looked around. Forest Woman was pointing at his booth.

"Thought we'd lost you there, ha ha… You got some visitors. These boys here, they really want to talk to you!"

Oh, more interested youngsters. When he looked over at the three boys milling around by his booth and grinning ear-to-ear they didn't remind him of Roy Wayne Byce so much, though. The stocking caps and striped sweaters made sense he supposed but, big torn-up short pants – and in the winter? All that shaggy black hair, red high top sneakers, flannel shirts tied around their waists, two of them even with visible tattoos: well, they weren't 4-H-ers. What's more, they were appreciating it, but not in a way he liked: they were… *enjoying* it.

He wouldn't exactly have called them "boys" either. BUT, you can't judge a book… so he put on his best shake and howdy face.

"Eve'nin' there young men. So… ya here ta see the work?"

"The work... Oh, yeah! Yeah, you know it man!" said the short, energetic "boy" with the ear spools. He looked around at his cohorts and they all laughed a hearty, red-eyed laugh. "Yeah, we drove all the way down from Athens!"

"So stoked dude! Right, Toby?" said the tall kid in a NASCAR shirt.

"Heavens, that's quite the pilgrimage!" Ansel said, nearly blushing. "I'm... well, flattered I reckon."

"Dude, we saw this in *Flagpole* and saw it was here and so Logan and Jared and me said we have *got* to go see this thing," Toby explained.

Ansel flinched a little. There was that "thing" word again. Still, he gushed, "Well, we're mighty glad an' proud ya'll could come on down all this way ta hear the message."

Toby, who had done most of the talking, looked around as if to see whom the "we" was, then said, "It's got a message? Cool. You push a button or something?"

"A real message. His written Word, an' its message a Hope an' freedom from Fear..."

Ansel tried to hand him a brochure to further their enlightenment but then all they wanted to do was take pictures. They took pictures of the work in action from various angles, then handed Ansel the camera. Toby instructed him to "just

The Work

push that button right there, dude" and, after Ansel – for safety – snapped toggle switch to "off," they started posing and mugging all around it. All three stood behind it with their arms over one another's shoulders and beaming, then they all took a knee at the front, shot peace signs or made the UT "hook 'em horns" – which Ansel thought odd for students from Georgia – and stuck out their tongues.

They asked Forest Woman to come take some pictures of them with Ansel. Which she did with a barely perceptible sigh. For these they all stood straight with faux good and proper stiffness and serious faces. Either Jared or Logan – whichever was the one who had so far done nothing but laugh, poked out his lower lip, half-closed his swollen eyelids and placed his hand on his gut like Napoleon. When they had finished, Forest Woman silently dropped the camera back in the tall one's hand and slowly walked, wooden-faced, but dolphin-smiling, back across to her booth.

"So... this is all, like, hunters and farmers here and crap like that?" Toby asked, bouncing his head like bobble doll.

Ansel, throwing the toggle back to "on" and beginning to get stressed about these exotic and unaccountable youth, agreed, "Yes. Farmers, hunters... you, you mus' be a hunter too I reckon... from your shirt."

"What?" the young man said looking down at his breast.

"Slayer," Ansel said. "That what that's about?"

"AWWWWWEESSOOMMMME! Hey dudes, you hear that? Oh man, I am so loving this!"

They all giggled.

Ansel, understanding less and less and "loving this" least of all, continued – but now trying to redirect the youth's attention away from the work and from himself – rambling on, "An' well, let's see... an' she, she over there, she... she grows pine cones an'..."

"Grows pine cones!? hahahahaha!" Toby guffawed. "Are you freakin' kidding me? Pine cones? Ohhh, man...This is the *best* night of my life, dude! For what? You mean for, like, Christmas stuff?"

In the midst of the unfolding chaos, the silent one who had aped Napoleon began reading the brochure out loud. "blah blah... 'serpent emerging from the weeds beyond the roadway's edge...' blah blah 'strewn with the refuse of sin...' *oh, man...* 'liquor bottle, cigare-...' Hey! That's a map of New York City. What the hell, man? My family's from New York... *butt*head... blah blah...'asphalt, his natural habitat... pure and level as the Lord,' hahaha '... solid as Man's dominion over Nature... the armadillo Michael...' What?? His name is *Michael?* The

The Work

armadillo is named Mike! hahahaha What the... *heeheehahahahahhaee!!!"*

Ansel grabbed the brochure sputtering, "It ain't his *name!* It... HE *re-pre-sents* the archa-..." he looked at the brochure and his heart sank when he now, for the first time, realized he had neglected to write, "representing the archangel" in the copy he took to Kinko's, so it actually was just an armadillo named Michael.

NASCAR, chuckling, stepped up and yelled out "Dude, Toby... what he said about you being a hunter – they'd never let you, man... 'cause... 'cause no one would *arm-a-dildo*!!! Boooyah!"

"Word!"

They all slapped palms like chimps as Ansel stood staring into the void and began to anxiously rub his forehead, forcing his false hair free of its adhesive and his crown.

"Hey bro," NASCAR interjected, chuckling like a jackhammer, "what do you think my shirt 'means'? snort..."

They all cracked up again.

While from deep within asking for help, on the outside Ansel began to call out, like a medium reporting from the spirit world, the neon green, yellow and pink words before him upon the field of black cotton-poly blend on the tall kid's chest.

"'Kyle Petty'... 'Mello Yello'... 'Forty Two'..." then looked him in the eye, "a fan...?"

"Yeah, no, I didn't even know who he was 'til the song came out. You know that one? Soundgarden... 'Kyle Petty, Son of Richard?'

> *"Heat is risin' feelin' high an' I'm on my wayyy*
>
> *Tell me if you wanna take a HIT!*
>
> *Right beside you, came to fight so get outta ma way*
>
> *'Cuz Daddy told me don't you ever take no fuckin' SHIIIIIT!!!"*

Yeah!"

He scrunched his face up, bit his lower lip and went into a wild air guitar solo.

> *"DERDALADERDALA*
>
> *WAHWAHWAHRRRAYYYRRRAYYYRRR*
>
> *WAHWAHAHDERDALDERDALA*
>
> *WAHWAHHHHHH – Yeah!!*

"You don't know this, man?

> *"... Daddy didn't raise no fuckin' fool!'"*

Forest Woman started to walk across the aisle.

> *"Well, comin' up on your right!*

The Work

Comin' up on your right!

Comin' up on your right no one's gonna

FUCK with me TONIIIIIGHT!!!'

"Yeah! Really? C'mon...

'"... Gonna get ta you,

gonna get ta youuuu...'

"Great fuckin' song, man. Should totally listen to it..."

Ansel, rubbing his temples with both hands now, pushed his hairpiece up to flop off to one side of his head as Forest Woman put her hand on NASCAR's shoulder.

"Well, you boys must have a long drive back up to Athens," she said with the authority of bar bouncer "and it's getting late, so maybe it's time you got going. Okay?"

"We're not going back to Athens." NASCAR objected. "Logan's old man's with the Guard. We're staying in Warner Robins..."

"Well, you don't hafta go home, you just hafta leave."

Toby looked at her shirt, "Roquefort? You mean like *cheese? hahaha* I thought you made *decorations* lady..."

"Alright. Let's go asswipes." She shoved Toby backwards and worked NASCAR into some kind of professional wrestling submission hold in about two seconds. She got both moving towards the door while the survivalist Richard stood and watched like a wooden Indian from his booth.

Forest Woman outweighed any two of them together by forty pounds but NASCAR was wiry and twisted hard, yelling "get your hands *off* me *BITCH!*" then tumbled into the bear, taking the stuffed animal to the floor with him, where the beast's claws tore his arm and shredded his Kyle Petty shirt..

As Napoleon jogged out, Forest Woman pulled up NASCAR – who was whining, "Fuck! You fucking fucked up my fucking shirt! You fucking *fucks*!" – and dragged him like an unruly child to the big open overhead door while a group of less urban teenagers watched dumbfounded. Toby hopped backwards out of the building into the now heavy rain, yelling back, "Your shit looks fakey, asshole! Fucking bald-ass cracker!" and began singing the "*derder der der, der der, der der der*" of *Dueling Banjos* as he bounced out. After NASCAR had been given the bum's rush and the last of them disappeared into the darkness and the downfall and Forest Woman returned up the aisle to see to Ansel, Richard sprang into action, grabbing a red Muskogee war club from his arsenal, snatched up the scrap of NASCAR's shirt and, with a manly bow-legged stride, proceeded to the gate where he stood like Hercules.

Just then, young Roy Wayne Byce ran in soaked and excited about having won his hog contest. He loped along, then slowed to a cautious gate upon seeing Richard there with his cudgel, the bear on the floor, and Forest Woman up by Ansel, who stood in the aisle, appearing to be half-scalped, and staring like a zombie at a back corner of the Hall.

Roy Wayne walked along, trying to make sense of the evidence of some unknown cataclysmic event surrounding him. All around, man and beast stood or lay frozen like the plaster casts from volcanic ash of unfortunate Pompeians. The crackling and popping of the work was the only sound in the Hall. There appeared to be blood on the decumbent bear's claw.

"Mr. Bragg?"

Ansel came to quickly this time and found himself staring at the graphics in the booth to his right:

Sorghum:

Drought Crop of the Future!

"What is happenin'?" he said almost inaudibly through the dry and flakey fingers that squished his cheeks and lips. "What is it that's comin'?"

"Mr. Bragg?"

"... You're a... a fine young man Roy Wayne..." Ansel said to the sorghum.

"Yes sir."

"... How long, ye simple ones... the scorners delight in their scorning..." Ansel said to the unhearing sorghum, once more.

"Yes sir."

Ansel went on as if already in the middle of whispering a tale to some unseen listener. "I think. I *think* this here is over now," he said, still through his feeling-less fingers and squinting as if trying to make out something in the distance. "This evenin's over an' I... I reckon... well, I oughta get back ta the Rodeway Inn." He spoke from very far away. "I can't say I expected *this*. It's all so... new... diff'rent kinda new. A new new... Like that... The mornin'... Dag, it was *so hot* that year. Dry. The fields was *all* burnt up. Gone. All that red, cracked dirt looked like everthin' was... was just fields a broken flower pots... an' that mornin' we all lined up on th' Okgatalatchee that mornin' an' that mornin' – the sun was still low, comin' 'long 'cross the high grass on the edge there, an' all glowin' that mornin' – an' the bugs flyin' in the yella sun an' buzzin' an' clickin' in the grass... an' it jus' felt like, like some kinda windless wind, an' your heart just *burstin'*... That make sense? An' it felt like... Ya know...? ...Like you was... *still in Heaven*. Ya know... Ya know how... how they say babies r'all up there in Heaven before

The Work

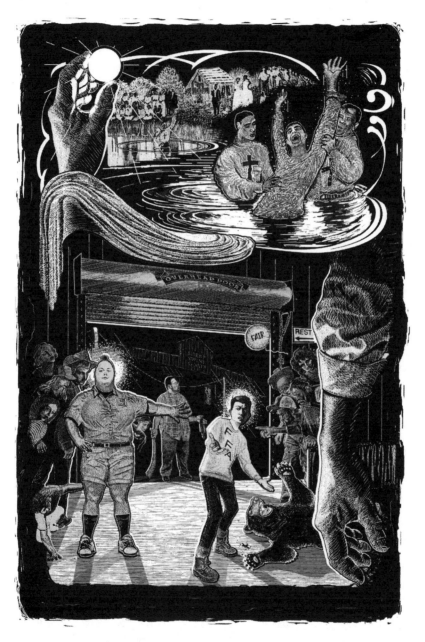

Like you was still in Heaven

they're born? How they come down from Heaven ta be born? *That's* how it felt like. Like you was up there. Like you was still in Heaven... like all them babies... I *know* what Heaven feels like. An' the water... cool... *cold*, an' when I come up with a mouthful a river... You had a mouthful a river Roy Wayne?"

"I... I don't think so Mr. Bragg."

"Oh an' when I come up jus' chokin' fine on th' Okgatalatchee... jus' a *coughin'* that river back up... wooo... it wudn't Heaven *no more*... No sir, hahahaha... But... But, yeah... But it was good. It was good. It was jus'... new. It's like that. But it ain't like that *at all*. Lord... My goodness... The Lord *does* cook in queer pots... Don' 'e?"

"Mr. Bragg?"

Ansel continued to no one but the sorghum, "If you're dead after ya die... what are ya *before* you're born? Like them babies... in Heaven. What would that be? What on Earth would ya even *call* that? ..."

"Mr. Bragg?"

"Uh huh?"

"You okay?"

"Yeah, Yeah... I just need ta get to the Rodeway Inn."

He walked towards the gate. One last gob of scalp glue still held the toupee to the side of his head where it flapped in rhythm as he trod out with the slouching shuffle of a man on a chain gang.

"Mr. Bragg?"

Ansel stopped and rotated slightly back. "Yes... Roy... Wayne?"

"I give away all a them brochures ya give me. *Ever* one of 'em."

Ansel pulled his face into a painful smile that creaked like a rusty door as it stretched, and with an imperceptible nod turned back to shuffle out into the rain past Richard who then, club in hand, cake-walked back to where Forest Woman and Roy Wayne stood.

"What happened? He seemed so... sad," Roy Wayne asked sorrowfully.

"He's weak," Richard barked.

"Yeah, Dick," Forest Woman sighed. "Yeah... Bless his heart."

•••

Ansel Bragg took his time motivating that morning. He stayed at the Rodeway Inn right up until checkout time. At the fairgrounds he picked up the work and the box marked,

"Miscellaneous Stuff," he kept under the folding table and which someone had thoughtfully repacked and overlapped the alternating flaps to close it up tight.

He had no eager youth to help him today.

Ansel looked around the Hall and it was all as it had been before the incident. He noticed how the quiet of the big room was like a sound itself. He noticed how the slightest sound echoed in a sinister way.

•••

The Work

X

On the way to Cordele Ansel stopped at the Waffle House on I-75, had Cheese n' Eggs, hash browns scattered and smothered, a side of patty sausage and nursed his coffee through three refills. He drove for almost two hours with his mind a blank until outside Albany, long after he'd exited the interstate, when he saw a sign for Radium Springs and thought, if he could, he would like to get the thing unloaded this afternoon. He gripped the wheel hard, realizing what he had just called the work.

Holding the Road Atlas against the wheel with both hands, Ansel attempted to navigate and drive at the same time. After a while he had managed, he thought, to narrow it down to the proper neighborhood until the level of detail and unnamed surface streets on the tiny map of Albany in the corner of the page for the whole state rendered it useless. He stopped for directions at the Radium Springs Atomik Mart where the man behind the counter said he thought that that church wasn't actually *in* Radium Springs but just *on* Radium Springs Road, which was a big road and went a long way up north into Albany itself. Frustrated, but with no choice, Ansel Bragg returned to the truck and began to travel up Radium Springs Road which was, as the clerk had said, a divided four lane with lots of traffic lights, and muffler shops, and cheap motels and not a few boarded-up businesses.

Seeing some kids in big coats and hoods on bicycles sitting in a vacant parking lot with tall dead weeds busting through the cracks, he pulled in and called them over to the truck.

"Say, you boys know where the... " he unfolded a piece

of paper from his pocket and read, "'the Radium Springs Church...' No... 'the Radium Springs Christ... *Christ Our Redeemer*... A... M... E... Church' is at?"

The boys looked at each other then, in unison, pointed in the same direction. One of them said, "Over't th' Moultrie road... what you doin' over *there?*"

"Oh, I... I just need ta deliver somethin.' So jus' up that a way?"

"Uh huh. Up yonder pass th' pawn shop. Got a big sign up th' front."

"Alright. Thank ya," and he took off.

It was right where the kids had said it would be. He parked in the gravel turnaround and got out to look around. There was a big sign on wheels out front with a flashing arrow and a marquee that read,

SUNDAY 1l AM 5ERVICE

"HERE COMES THE JUDGE,

4ERE COME S THE JUDGE"

REV. JOHN WESL3Y RAIFORD

Ansel thought, "Well there's a good name for a

preacher". He wondered if the reverend was around so he could get the thi... the work... set up. He thought the Black man in the old sweatshirt raking leaves out of the foundation planting at the side of the building might know and called out "Say there! Say you... Yeah, yeah you... Say, ya know where this preacher... *Raiford*'s at?"

The man stood straight and, with his rake, assumed the parade-rest position of a military rifle corpsman and said, "I... am the Reverend Raiford." with a deep, round and intimidating voice.

"Oh my goodness!" Ansel thought. "This is a... *colored* church."

"Do you have some bus-i-ness you wish to conduct?" the daunting Reverend Raiford went on.

"Oh, dear... My name is... Ansel. Ansel Bragg. I'm bringin' the... the... sculpture. Th'*Armadilla dee-vruntun Rattlesnakeo*," he said, failing in his panic to remember that he had never actually used those words as its title, nor had anyone, ever, for any reason used them.

"*You* are Ansel Bragg?"

"Yes... Reverend..."

The Work

"I expected someone..." he took a deep breath, "Well! ...Let us move forward!"

The awkward first meeting aside, they attained a not uneasy symbiosis and worked together to struggle with the work from the truck, up the stairs, and place it upon a card table in the narthex covered with a royal purple cloth.

As they stood wiping their brows after the chore was completed, the Reverend had to admit that the person he expected to see was, "...a man of color."

"I could have gone either way just with that name of yours, but, well... to the *African* Methodist Episcopal Church, most certainly." But now, upon reflection, he felt humbled believing Ansel Bragg to be a man of goodwill and was pleased that the Lord had brought them together as brothers in Christ. "We are all the same under the skin. But then, you must know that as well as anybody."

Ansel, though working sincerely to adjust, nodded in agreement, but was truly thinking how, oftentimes, skins alone made difference enough.

•••

Before service on Sunday, after Ansel arrived at the church from the Rodeway Inn, he brought in the cardboard "miscellaneous" box from the truck and opened it to retrieve an extension cord. When opened, he could not miss seeing a Chock Full o'Nuts coffee can within: stuffed with money. He pulled it out and looked it over. How had he come to have a can of money? Someone else's... *can of money*? He hadn't packed the box, so someone else had made this mistake. But who, and how and... a *can-of-money*?

He pulled out the wadded bills and change to count and it was almost seventy-five dollars.

There was also a business card.

Diana Bodeker

Chief Forester, Eatonton Seed Orchard

Georgia – la Roquefort Corp.

Forest Products • Pharmaceuticals • Industrial Solvents

Atlanta, GA • Eugene, OR • Rodez, France

They had collected money. For him? For what? Because of those kids? There was no damage done.

He felt humiliated. Was he some pathetic character that needed to have bills slipped into his pocket, unaware, by pitying

The Work

do-gooders to make his way less appalling and miserable? It had only made it more so.

Ansel walked away squeezing the bottom half of his face with one hand and slapping the stack of bills against his thigh with the other. He stopped and composed himself. He reminded himself that *he* had not extracted this pity tribute. He had picked himself up – after a mild meltdown – then had continued on his Godly mission without question or pause. All such missions are fraught with tribulation and anyone taking on such a task should know and be prepared for thus.

Ansel returned the shame money to the can, flicked off the toggle so the work wouldn't disturb the service, plugged in the cord, then rocked his head side-to-side like a boxer readying himself in his corner, straightened his tie, tugged down on the bottom of his suit coat and headed towards the nave with re-born courage. And besides, Black people were starting to come in and he didn't want to be caught in this vestibule having to explain himself.

Ansel sat in a corner on the back row of Christ our Redeemer. The Reverend Raiford had requested he sit in the front as guest of honor, but he was much too humble to accept that kind of honor or attention, or capable of having that many people behind him. Still, he got attention nonetheless. Every parishioner who walked in the door took notice of him. He was taken aback how nearly every man, woman and (compelled) child made a point to walk to the lonely corner where he sat and welcome him to the service. Most shook his hand. Particularly the children, sternly told to "take that man's hand and *welcome* him!" after which, with his big pale, flakey hand in theirs they would flatly sing "*Well*-cumm," without making eye contact.

During the service the Reverend devoted a good twenty minutes to praise of, and long exegesis on, the profound symbolisms of the work. Each praise or pointing out of some manifestation of the Lord's Word made real in the work was followed by heads turned to one another, a general murmur of agreement and smiling faces turning in their pews to nod with approval and gently exclaim some hosanna towards Ansel. He could scarcely believe how much vocal interaction – *conversation* – occurred throughout the service between the Reverend Raiford, the congregation, and God. Even when Hazel's sister had briefly hooked up with that bunch of strychnine drinkers and snake handlers over near Lumber City there hadn't been as much chatter. And, anyway, that was mostly just screaming.

At the end the Reverend remarked upon his favorite and "most thoughtfully revealed of the semiotics incorporated into

The Work

this most penetrating and sagacious work of Christian philosophy."

       ...and, to mine own eyes, the statement made, whereby from the loss of the mightiest and most *powwwwerful* support known – that from *ON HIGH!*... that loss represented in the guise of the top bolt of the sign – removed, lost, *taken away!* And making thus to fall, the *SIGN – pointing DOWNward!! That sign* with its representation of a curving road and the many dangers implied therein, *THAT sign...* upon whose face we see also revealed in the form of the dangerous, curving road... the *very image* of the serpent... ...

       ... ... the serpent and the sin he brought, through the weakness of woman, upon the world... sin which could be redeemed... even by Satan *himself* through the blood of our Savior *Jesus of Nazareth!* Whereby we here see that only if one *remains* vigilant against the loss of God's support can we *be SAVED...* Is the most *profound and*

enlightening statement of all... ... ...
Ultimately, and through an ironic symbolism, we see *THAT sign...* that bullet-riddled sign, portends *the defeat of Satan.* Defeat through the actions of our *warriors against* him and the forces of evil and *im*-mo-rality!

"Wow!" thought Ansel. And each and every point had been punctuated with a chorus of "Amen!" "Yes Lord, yes Lord, Yes!" and "PraiseGodPraiseGod *Praise GOD!!*"

Now a floor tom and electric bass began a slow heartbeat. Then along with the – to Ansel, almost menacing – march, pulsing chords from a pumping Hammond B3 organ began and the congregation clapped along with the steady beat. The Reverend Raiford picked up a microphone and began to chant,

"Hal-le-luuu, Ohhhhhh Hal-le-luuu!"

The congregation sang along,

"Hal-le-luuuuuuAuuu-jah!"

Then they all sang,

"You know the storm is passing over,

Hal-le-lu!"

And on and on, over and over, and Ansel thought this

The Work

The storm is passing over
Hallelujah

was not at all like the songs in his church, even as he failed to notice his hand tapped along with the rhythm.

The congregation took over the refrain, and never thereafter let up, as the Reverend took the lead with a rafter shaking baritone,

"Take courage my soul and let us journey on,
Though the night is dark and we're far from home.
You know the storm is passing over,
Hal-le-lu!"

The song went on and on and soon Ansel was far away in trance, swaying to the music. The storm was passing, Ansel was safe, God was good...

"Ya know, some folks turning back, God doesn't turn back!"
the Reverend admonished,

"Who's that yonder, dressed in black?"

and deep inside, Ansel felt his insecurities squirm a little.

"Look like a man who turn'd his back"

One of the congregation called out, "You better *sang* that song!!" and Ansel shot to his feet, eyes wide open, as he always assumed all scolds were directed at him.

He was not out of place on his feet now, among the swaying, clapping, and chanting parishioners. The few that even

The Work

noticed his bolting from the pew merely nodded with affirmation and wide grins of approval. Ansel stood for the remainder of the song, still swaying, unaware, from his transcendent moment's residual wave action. When it all ended, he stood alone in his corner nervously straightening his tie and popping the bottom of his suit coat – though oddly exhilarated.

As the congregation filed out to view the work – each member once more greeting him with warmth and a sincere smile as they passed – Ansel resolved himself to feeling OK about the fact that, even though the whole thing with the bolt was a result of it having vibrated loose on the road, fallen out and rolled into a gap in the GMC Sierra's bed near the wheel well where he would never find it, he was going to go ahead and take credit and run with it. Those vibrations and poor nut-torqueing were surely part of the Lord's plan.

At last he drifted to the narthex portal, hardly able to enter for the crowd gathered there, but from the flashing and popping he could tell that Reverend Raiford had flipped the toggle. He took a deep breath and waded in. As he waded, hands were clapped upon his back and heartfelt compliments followed by "brother" were liberally handed out. And, oh my, they were so *well-dressed*. Each and every one of them in finery he had not seen in a congregation since his youth. From the freshest infant to the most antediluvian of elders, the cut, the material, the accessories and accoutrements of their habiliments were exceeding.

While still attempting to squirm his way to the front of the crowd and to his handiwork, which the group was admiring, an elderly woman – as finely attired as any and with a regal dignity – touched his arm with a tiny hand gloved in the same white dress gloves his mother had once worn to assembly so many years ago.

"Such a wonderful thing, young man. It does you proud and brings glory to the Lord. Bless you," she said, with bright eyes that sparkled through the tulle veil of her little black hat. She squeezed his hand in her small, frail one as she raised it to her lips and pecked lightly upon its back. She then turned, and with assistance and a slightly unsteady walk, moved away through the crowd that parted for her.

She stopped for a moment, as if in thought, then turned back to say, "You know, young man... you would receive a great many more donations if you was to put the collection plate up high, where folks could see it." She smiled once more, then turned and continued out the door through the pathway the faithful held for her.

Ansel didn't know what that meant until, turning back

The Work

to the work and moving closer, he saw that the Chock Full
o'Nuts can, still on the floor in the box he had not closed after
his pre-sermon episode, was now stuffed with even more money:
so much so that it overflowed the can with flat and crumpled
bills raining down into the box, filling it and covering the
rubber-banded bundles of his brochures of shame.

"Good *Godamighty!*" he blurted out in nothing but
shock.

"Amen!" rang out all around him. "God is great!"

"Not again!" he agonized. Then he paused in thought:
this was different. This wasn't a collection taken in secret out of
some misplaced compassion to soften the blow of his having
been mocked by youths. This was benefaction given freely in
appreciation of the work. These were monetary blessings
conferred probably in direct proportion to the spiritual benefit
received from viewing the work.

"God *is* great..."

Ansel knew there was nowhere to stay in Omega, so he
was compelled to spend another night in Albany, but was, this
night, invited, and accepted, to be a guest in the home of the
Reverend Raiford and his wife Euodia; of whom, by the next

morning, he had come to comfortably refer to with her husband's pet diminutive as "Yoodie." That same morning he accepted – welcomed – the Reverend's big bear embrace as he departed early for the Omega school and embarked upon his voyage with a warm new optimism.

•••

When Ansel turned onto the Ty Ty Omega Road and looked down the long stretch of road under the gray sky, he felt at ease and sang, lowly, not even realizing it or moving his lips as he drove, but, still, he sang,

"Talk about me, much as ya please,

But more ya talk, I gonna bend my knees

Hal-le-luuuuuuAuuu-jah!"

and the miles of flat farmland again set his mind to contemplation. The great expanses of dormant fields awaiting their spring eruptions of cotton and peanuts caused him to meditate once more upon the notion of seed and growth and renewal. The miles of wheeled mechanical apparatus of the center-pivot irrigation systems dozing quietly along the

The Work

roadside, waiting to awaken and pump the pure water from the ancient marine sedimentary deposits of the Pleistocene and Holocene Ages (or as Ansel would say "flood times") of the Coastal Plain surficial aquifer and force the crops to emerge and be made plump and green, was likened unto the Holy Spirit flowing through and over the God-fearing that they be quenched of desire, grow to promote His glory, and be ready to accept His promise at harvest time.

Then, looking at the gray skies overhead, he thought, "looks like long 'bout supper time might come a shower a rain… that'd water them crops." So man's machinations were really unneeded…

His deep, endless and self-contradictory metaphorizing continued until he pulled into the parking lot of the Gen. Raymond G. Davis Combined School of Omega.

Principle Margie Hornbuckle met him and had the janitor help him move the work into the cafetorium where it was placed on the floor between the small stage and the dining tables. He then had about an hour before the students would begin to stream in for lunch in which to prepare some short presentation.

There was a time, not too long ago, when the prospect of giving any sort of public address, much less one so impromptu, would have disabled Ansel's brain. But now, after having made so many little speeches, *ad libs* and interpretations, and after hearing so many other gifted speakers like the Reverends Bullock and, good Lord, Raiford, philosophize upon the work he felt more than up to the task of mesmerizing a bunch of eight year-olds for five or six minutes.

As the children began to come in, at first with their minds only on getting their milk and cream corn and meat loaf, they soon were drawn like moths to a flame by the bizarre and exciting display at the far end of the room. Unable to resist the magnetic pull of something involving snakes and bullet holes and grandly aggressive, be-caped, armadillos – if they even knew what it was – they soon milled about, jockeying for a better view, three to four deep.

Miss Hornbuckle clapped her hands as if summoning a genie and commanded that they all take a seat so Mr. Bragg could tell them a thing or two about the work. There would then be time for a closer viewing followed by a slightly longer than usual time to finish their dinners and return to class.

When Ansel began his little talk he followed the tropes of his usual homily. But as he rambled on, his monologue became discursive, then settled – without his even being completely aware – onto the topic of the human tendency to see

The Work

good in the familiar and evil in the unknown. Seeming, to the children – who looked to one another with amusement and knitted brows – to be thinking out loud, he mused on about there being all kinds of people in the world, and that among each of these many kinds were to be found many good, many not-so-much and many just misguided individuals, and those were even to be pitied.

He then began to wax therapeutic that perhaps his own past lack of recognition – or appreciation – of this incontrovertible Nature of the Mankind of God's making was perhaps the reason he had found more security among animals, and even then dead ones, among which he now realized he had hidden, rather than walk in confidence and Love among the rainbow of the equally admirable, equally failed, yet equally created brotherhood of Man...

Realizing he had wandered deep into the weeds, he paused just long enough to correct his course, finished with a brief but riveting climax which encouraged the children to "*be* the armadillo, wear the armor the Lord give ya an' kick Satan's hind quarters" and, finally, the Lord loves you.

Once again the children returned to buzz around the work like bees on a honeysuckle bush, and were largely respectful, even asking a few thoughtful questions. There is, of course, Ansel thought, "always the one wisenheimer," as the chubby kid – the obvious class clown, with a broken front tooth from which, for some reason, wires emerged – began to sing – alone, then along with the rest of the class as they became infected –

"Jesus love me, this I know
Th'arm-a-dill-o tell me so."

This brought an end to the presentation and Miss Hornbuckle clapped her hands once more, now commanding the students get in line with their trays. This didn't stop the children's choir, but it did move it further away as Ansel began to pack up the work, again with the help of the janitor, whose name he bothered to learn.

On the rest of the trip home, Ansel worked from one end of the anxiety spectrum to the other. On the one hand, this trip had been enlightening: profitable even.

"I mean, colo-... *Black* folks gave *me* money," he thought; shaking his head in giddy befuddlement.

Not to mention the students who had dropped their

The Work

lunch money in the can that, this time, he had – not so secretly, and with seed money in the bottom – put "up high."

On the other hand, there had been awful, awful things: humiliations and mockery. But, as he had thought before, that was part of the deal when spreading the Gospel in such a boots-on-the-ground way. And the Radium Springs church had been so nice. But then again, so were the people in Perry who had apparently only pitied him.

Did *everybody* really only pity him? Some only hiding their pity with pretend support? Like with that stage hypnotist he and Hazel had seen at that casino in Mobile he had thought it sinful even to enter. But that deceiver's victims from the audience: Ansel was certain they knew him to be a fraud. One woman had even reached back to pull her shirttail down to cover her behind – which was peeking above her pants as she bent down – while supposedly under the mesmerer's spell. "I mean, C'mon..." People, he thought, would rather publicly cluck like chickens and run around as if their pants were on fire than humiliate one they knew to be a charlatan claiming to be in control; would rather acquiescently surrender their own dignity and free will, shaming themselves, to maintain the fiction of a superior power...

He felt himself slipping into some sort of blasphemy and stopped thinking.

•••

The Work

XI

"You *cain't* be serious."

"I am. I told ya, big things," a nearly jubilant Ansel proclaimed. "They're a-comin' Haze, I tell ya..." and he danced a little jig and clapped his hands together. "An' now with Springfield an' the contest... I tell ya the Lord's a-workin' behind the scenes."

"Well, I wish He'd come work in the shop some. 'Cause things is gettin' *tight*, Anse. An' you swore – *swore* – you was gonna slow down and get back ta business after all a this."

"I am, really. Just gonna do Springfield an' maybe a few more churches. 'Ventually I gotta give the thi... *it*... back to Mullis. Or give 'im back his hundred dollars. But look a-here..." he picked up the Chock Full o'Nuts can, pulled out a rubber banded roll of bills and shook it as if expecting it to rattle. "Look, Haze. Three hundred an' *forty*-three *dollars*."

"What's that?"

"Money. Money they give me."

"*Give* you?"

"Yeah."

"Who? Why?"

"People. Everybody. Just because. I don't even ask. I *wouldn't* ask. They just... a-want ta. See?"

"Oh, I don't know." Hazel seemed frazzled. "This is just all crazy... Well, at least we can keep the bed now. Which I won't be in for a while, by the way."

"Why not?"

"I'm stayin' out ta the camp with Norma."

"I ain't seen you at all in four days, Haze. An' hardly at all in... months, seems like."

"I know... but she's tired a the kids and Robert ... and I reckon I need to get away and think some too..."

"Think...? Oh... Aw'right. I guess... Can't stay out ta the camp though."

"Why not?"

"Still a-got them bees in the wall..."

"Don't bees sleep in the winter? Well, anyways, whatever, we'll take Norma's truck so we can sleep out, in case. Be fun I reckon. Ohh my Lord... Anyways, Dr. Pirkle called, wants you to see 'im."

The Work

"Oh... Okay... Haze...?"

"Mmmm?"

"...Ya know, there's still some fish down in Bartram's Hole... what say one Sunday you an' me go devil 'em?"

"Ohh, Anse... you ain't got time..."

...

XII

Dr. Pirkle seemed friendly enough but had an all-business air to his greeting. "I'm glad you're back, Anse, and I'm glad ya come in right away."

96

The Work

"Dang Alvin, that don't sound... promisin'."

"Again, don't go gettin' your britches in a twist. What it is... what they *say* it is, is real easy to cure. The disease that is. May be some complications with your nerves they may want to do some work on. But gettin' rid a it's easy as pie, I'm told."

"*Disease?* I got a disease?"

"Yes, it's a disease. It's what I thought it might be before. And this *can* get right serious, but it's curable easy, just kinda strange ta get it at all, but it's slow... takes a good while ta show. That's why I wondered... Anyway, they got all kinds a medicines wrap it right up quick now, but I want you ta go up to Em'ry in Atlanta get checked out... get the pills and have 'em talk about the nerve stuff with ya. Some special treatment they want ta try."

"Oh Lord. Why *now?* ...But what is it? What's it called?"

"It's... uh... it's somethin' called 'Hansen's disease.'"

"Hanson's disease? Never heard a that."

"Didn't figure ya had."

After leaving the office Ansel went straight to the camp to tell Hazel about what Dr. Pirkle had said. She and her sister were sitting in lawn chairs under a tarp drinking beer.

Unfortunately so was Norma's common-law husband, Robert Riddle Duquesne: Bobby. Or, less to his own liking, his childhood nickname, "Dookie."

Bobby sat slouched in a lawn chair with a can of beer on his stomach and wearing a tank top. At least he was wearing a shirt at all. He was usually shirtless and looked like everybody who had ever been arrested on *Cops*. He was from a fairly well-known and − to everyone's general agreement − awful, white trash clan that lived in a collection of trailers and shacks on the dirt road that ran along Rangle's Branch near the county line off the winding Vico Road. They had once had some property and a decent-sized hog farm but sloth and indolence had finally taken over causing them to lose the whole thing, save that one parcel in the floodplain.

Norma had tried to justify her common-law's cruel, stupid and violent ways to her sister as being tied to some horror from the last days of his family's hog empire. The Duquesne's had three large and vicious bulldogs used to control the hogs. These dogs were, it was claimed, so savage and unpredictable that they had to have massive, cumbersome wooden manacles locked around their wrists to slow them, so that a man might outrun them had they gone off and tried to chase him down and kill him. One night, one of the dogs loosed his fetters and ran

The Work

down Robert's drunken father – the undisputed tyrant ruler of the clan – overtaking, then mangling him as he fled, finally hobbling him such that the remaining handcuffed beasts caught up to him. In his efforts to escape he had fallen – or jumped – into the hog pen, shredded and bloody, whereupon the swine finished the job the dogs had begun, making trough fodder of the stewed pater familias.

Apparently, Bobby himself had found him, or what remained, the next morning. This consisted largely of some clothing and three feet: two of his and one rabbit's foot that the old man apparently carried in his pocket for good luck, along with a buckeye and a lump of what looked like rose quartz, which the younger Duquesne still kept with him and sometimes used to bust up rocks of crystal meth. This trauma, it was argued, had shattered his will to work and to not be perpetually wasted nor just generally odious. He was now only competent for work as a part-time flagman on highway crews: if that.

This was a sad story, even if untrue, but remembering how the whole Duquesne clan had joked that the Old Man was "jus' pig shit ta begin with, so… etc., etc." and looking at that old curmudgeon's begat now, almost completely melted into the nylon webbing of the lawn chair and picking at a constellation of face scabs, Ansel could not help but think there had *always* been plenty wrong with Dookie.

Now Ansel was sort of common-law related to him through Norma and was sort of common-law uncle to their son Randy and daughters Rhona and Rondell, to whom their father referred as "the two little split tails."

When Ansel drove up they all looked a little disappointed to see him, particularly Hazel's sister and even more so Robert. Their earlier business dealing aside, neither Bobby nor Ansel could stand the other.

Ansel said, "Hey" to his wife and by extension to the group.

Hazel said, "How you doin' Anse?"

Norma picked at a scab.

Dookie made a lazy "'s'up Bragg..." then lazed on, "y'all need ta do sumthin' 'bout 'em bees in'em walls 'ere..."

"I know Robert... but, not 'zactly top a m'list right now..."

"I don't be-*lieve* it you ne'ssarily need ta do nothin' 'bout it *yoursef*, Bragg..."

Ansel hated the way he just called him "Bragg."

"Ya know, they got 'em 'ere *en*-ter-*mola*-gists over ta the ag station over 'ere Tifton. An' I be-*lieve* they come over, take 'em bees outt'em walls on the state's dime. Ya know?" He

The Work

pushed a greasy strand of long hair off of his face so Ansel could see the smirk he made in appreciation of his own approximate knowledge of the word "entomologist."

"Yes, well, I will certainly look inta that first chance I get, Bobby..."

He excused his wife and himself from her sister and brother-in-common-law and they walked a little ways off down the leafy dirt road.

"Dang Haze, what the heck is *Dookie* doin' here? Thought she wanted ta get *away* from him."

"I don't know. They was both here when I come along. And they was already goin' at it. Least *she* was. She was realllly just givin' him up the country."

"Good Lord..."

"But then they both just shut up an' sit down, so I don't know... But what's goin' on Anse? What happened with the doctor? Things okay?"

"He thinks... I maybe got somethin' called 'Hanson's disease'"

"Lord, that sounds serious. Is that serious? Sounds serious."

"No. Well, it *can* be, but he says they'n cure it okay."

"Lemme see your hands."

He held them out as if about to be handcuffed.

"Dang, Anse. 'Zat what that is? Looks like that ol' armadilla."

"More like the snake."

They stood there for a while not saying anything.

At last Ansel said, "Well... I just stopped by, let ya know. Gonna head on ta the house. I reckon... Let ya be... I'll see ya. Love ya Haze."

"You too babe. Bye."

"*Oh*... I'm s'posed ta go up t'Atlanta. Up t'Em'ry hospital for my pills and whatnot..."

"*Annnse!* This jus' gets scarier and scarier, I swear. You tellin' me everything?"

"Yeah. It ain't nothin' Haze. Really. Jus' where they got the pills."

They walked along hand-in-hand, Hazel holding his unknowing one until they separated near the truck, when, pulling away toward the camp, she let it go to drop to his side.

Robert yelled out, "*Bragg!* 'Zit true you'uz a-hangin' at a *spook* church? Sleepin' 'ere?"

Ansel stopped as he pressed his thumb to the door handle button, opened his mouth to respond to Bobby, then shook his head, climbed in, cranked the engine, exasperatedly

The Work

mumbled, "*Dookie...*" then drove off down the road in a flurry of leaves. Hazel walked back to where her sister sat with a beer. She pulled one from the cooler for herself, popped the top and sat back in her chair.

"You ever hear a *Hanson's* disease?"

"No."

"Don't figure nobody has."

The next day at the real estate office where she worked, Norma went to the computer and typed, "hansons diseese" into Alta Vista. A moment later a blue list dropped down.

At the top of the page it said, "redirected to: Hansen's Disease – Leprosy."

•••

Within two days everyone in Utinahica knew Ansel Bragg had leprosy. Including Ansel Bragg. Not that anybody knew that for sure yet, but people always know the worst about others. People were avoiding him and the few people he considered friends were, apparently, not.

But right now he had bigger worries.

He had leprosy.

Things were real real, new new and different different now.

Now.

•••

The Work

Part 2

JD Hollingsworth

The Work

XIII

No one would do any sort of business with Ansel Bragg anymore.

People crossed the street when they saw him coming or ducked into doorways, only to poke their heads out after he passed to watch him – their faces puckered in a rictus of fear and disgust – then turn to one another and jabber away.

Sheriff Purdue, with a blatant lack of stealth, shadowed Ansel from the safety of his Crown Victoria cruiser as he walked the streets.

No mail was delivered.

No utility bill checks were touched, much less cashed.

No fallen game was pulled from the back of a bloody pickup for him to resurrect and, barren of lively fire, the gun range sat deathly silent.

At Strickland's Diner, the coffee he ordered from Laurlene Williams, like every previous morning, and always drank at the counter, was made "to go" and "on the house" as Laurlene struggled with a nervous smile while frantically waving off the dollar bill he attempted to hand her as if it was a vampire bat.

"Swear... Y'money ain't no good here! *No good!!*" she sputtered.

Ansel kicked at the half dollar the old coots in the corner booth had glued to the floor by the register and stomped out, angry and ashamed.

Children fled or remained only to throw rocks and the drunks made songs about him.

Alone and forsaken, it seemed the sound of a mournful wind and blowing trash followed him all his days.

The Work

Perhaps worst of all was to hear of the stories told of him: bawdy and gothic legends of how he had come to contract the Biblical scourge. "Remember them nights – *weeks* – we seen his light burning deep inta the night," they agreed with terror, like peasants in shivering huddles conspiring against Victor Frankenstein. "How he barely come out, even durin' the day, an' with his doors *allllways* bolted... So's we couldn't ketch'im!"

They could only imagine what unholy things he had been up to. And imagine they did, for as many tellers as there were to tell a tale was the number of tales told of perversions and crimes against nature of which he stood accused, and by each was he rendered to the lowly and repellant essence of the disease: "unclean," in all of its many meanings. With Hazel sequestered at the camp, Ansel knew of these tales through his one remaining lifeline to the world of the living: phone contact with Mullis Alewine, and by and by, even *he* would refuse to take Ansel's calls out of fear of infection, for sin's mysterious communicability could surely transmit through the line.

Were they right? Sinners get leprosy: punishment for those who displeased the Lord. That was Bible Truth. But it was also a simple illness, and one that could be easily cured. That was medical truth. Or so he was told. Dr. Pirkle could surely help him. Even if *he* couldn't *cure* the disease, he *could* reason with the town, inform them, ease their fears and take away Ansel's pain at being shunned.

The doctor let Ansel in the office, though his nurse, Louise, threw down her cigarette and took off out the back door when he came in. Dr. Pirkle told him there was nothing more he could do and that he should get up to the clinic in Atlanta and get this thing cleared up. Ansel pleaded that he was going to go to the clinic directly but that he needed to have him go to the town, to the people, and let them know, as a doctor, that this was just an illness, not a curse or moral affliction and that it would soon all be over and it would be safe to welcome him back into the heart and bosom of the community.

"I am a doctor Anse... And even to me it seems almost like some kinda reverse miracle what you ever got this. Regular, like a cold... And so, I'm also a deacon. And a Sunday school teacher... And I am sorry about your pain. But, shall we accept good from God, and not ol' trouble?" the doctor asked pointedly. "But ya know Anse... pain, well... pain is a *gift* from God. It's God's way a letting us know somethin's wrong. It's how we learn to not stick our hands in the fire... And there's all sorts a wrong and just as many kinds a pain the Lord's gifted us with to warn us away. We feel pain from sin *just as surely* as we

110

The Work

feel pain from hitting our thumb with a hammer. You've cut your hands up there because the Lord took away that pain. The pain that protected you. I don't know why He took it away... do you? And why did He bring this new pain, the pain a being turned away? Forsaken... Have ya though a what *you* might a *done?* And what *about* that pain He took *from* you. Don't ya miss that pain, Ansel? Don't ya want that pain? Wouldn't ya like to have your pain back, Anse?"

There was not enough numbness in the world to make him forget that the pain he knew now was plenty.

An empty Ansel left Dr. Pirkle's empty words to wander the empty streets. The only people he saw were Robert and a couple of the Winters boys leaning on their truck and drinking beer. They didn't run off but Bobby's middle finger made it clear he shouldn't approach either. Even Dookie was more welcome here than him.

What had he done? How had he offended God? The greatest thing he had ever accomplished in his entire life – created from his own mind, heart, and soul – was a powerful and honored work, inspired – *guided by* – and dedicated to the Lord, honoring and affirming His greatness and Ansel's complete devotion to Him. Had he not been *chosen* to create this for the

World? Would medicine even cure a pox sent by the Lord himself to smite someone who displeased Him?

There was only one place left to have *all* of these questions answered.

•••

The Reverend Pine stood holding his Bible on the porch, essentially blocking entrance to the church.

"There's kids inside. Daycare," the reverend rationalized.

"I know. I ain't gonna hurt nobody Reverend. I need some help... answers," Ansel pleaded, remaining in the dirt at the bottom of the steps.

"Answers?"

"I need to know *why* I got this. I need to know *if* I got it. Biblically. What ta do... I know there's tests the preacher can do an'... an' answers..."

"You're talking 'bout the Bible, Old Testament. Good Lord. I don't know about all these, all these... *'tests.'* I mean, I seen it here in Leviticus," he began flipping through the pages, "and all that about how... like here... how 'deep and raw' and" –

The Work

he swallowed deeply – "and, Good Lord, if your damn hair's turned white and... I mean, I *know* about it, I've read it for Christ's sake, but I ain't never 'spected to *need* this stuff. Who the Hell has to know that *now?* Besides you already *know*, I mean, Good Lord, Anse, they say you got it... the doctors." He moved a little further away. "I mean aside from that, I mean if you're looking for, what, a cure? *Here?* Hell, even Jesus only done it two times in the whole damn book. And, Good Lord, *that* was *Jesus*. Won't the doctors do it? I mean, can't they... they got stuff, prob'ly just pills or maybe just, like, some nose drops even."

"But you lay on hands. I seen. I thought you laid on hands..."

"Not *a leper!* Christ Almighty!"

"I need´ta be clean in the eyes a the Lord, Reverend. I seen ya heal folks...Jus' 'bout ev'ry Sunday."

"Well, uh, yeah, yeah Anse, sure... But, but well, that there... That was *regular* stuff. Ya know, some cripples, deaf folks, hammertoe... Stuff like that. Like I said, Jesus Himself only done this *twice*."

"You always said it wasn't you *doin'* the healin' anyways, but it *was* the Lord workin' *through* ya an' you was just like, was only the... the cable."

"Conduit, yeah sure, Anse. But they got doctors and all for this kinda stuff now. I mean this old timey stuff here it's like... like eating bacon, ya know?... We done... *overcome* that. Progressed to where bacon's *okay*. Ev'ry body eats bacon now, 'cept the Jews, but they got their own thing goin' on there and... but... it's okay now 'cause a science, and medicine I reckon. It's modern times, man. Bacon's okay. Ya know what I mean? And I think leprosy's... well, it's been licked by science, Anse, and I don't know what it needs a... a Christ-sized miracle or if the conduit's even the right... gauge for something like this. Hell, I don't even know f'it's the same... *BAC*-terium... as Bible days. Same disease... I don't think I can put my... that I can *lay hands on* and fix that. Doctors'll handle it. Have faith Anse. Have faith in Science."

"Oh. I see... can't lay *your* hands..."

"Don't be that way Anse..."

"I *am* that way."

"Hey Anse?"

"*What?*"

"Don't say nothin' 'bout... 'bout *this*... Okay?"

•••

The Work

XIV

I t took nearly two weeks to arrange an appointment at the Atlanta Hansen's Disease Clinic, and when that day came Ansel left the town that had left him out in the cold. Where he had now been cut off to the point of having to have food delivered and then only by Hazel, who would not herself enter the home or touch him, so just left the basket at the door like an unwanted child, and took off. So, though he hated cities with a passion, he could not get to Atlanta fast enough that day because Emory was now the only, the last, place left that he could be saved.

As he navigated the rat-king of highways into Midtown, Ansel recalled the family story of the only two times his grandfather, Jack, had ever left Torcall County: once to a clinic at Emory when he was ninety, and once with Pershing and the American Expeditionary Forces to France when he was seventeen. That was still funny, he thought: for some reason. He wasn't sure why, or even why it was a story.

He passed Crawford W. Long hospital and thought he remembered that name from his high school Georgia History class – how he had invented gassing people or something – then parked the truck in a pay lot, walked to Peachtree then down to number 550. He went in and read the menu board and found his way up to the clinic. When he checked in at the window he felt embarrassment, as if he actually had the donkey gonorrhea he had been accused of back in Utinahica. The receptionist didn't seem too worried to interact with him though, which was refreshing and, luckily, there weren't many lepers in Atlanta that day and so he was almost immediately called in to meet with a young doctor.

"Afternoon, Mr. Bragg, I'm Dr. Gary Nguyen. So, I

The Work

hear you have contracted a case of Hansen's."

"That is what I am told."

"Sure, sure. Well, uh, what I *can* tell you is that the skin biopsy we did on the sample sent by a..." he glanced down at his clipboard, "a Doctor *Pirkle*, indicated the presence of rod-formed, Gram-positive, and, through the Ziel-Neelsen and Fite-Faraco staining processes, acid-fast Mycobacterium bacilli, most assuredly Mycobacterium leprae because there are also the, uh, demarcated cutaneous lesions and loss of sensation that Doctor... uh... Pirkle described. And, uh, while I know that is just a bunch of hooey sounding nonsense to you, it does, to us, say that you do most likely have Hansen's. Disease. Now, uh, we'll need to run another test – the lepromin skin test – to confirm that you do indeed have the illness, and also its specific type and severity and, uh... Anyway, then you can probably rest assured that we can, uh, prescribe a simple regimen of antibiotics that should knock this out *tout de suite*. And one last thing..." Dr. Ngyuen hugged the clipboard to his chest and went on, "Uh, since you do seem to be showing evidence of some neuropathy in your extremities we would like to do a nerve biopsy to check on that and we were wondering – hoping – that you, uh, might be willing to participate in a new medical treatment. All voluntary of course, but we think it shows great promise."

"I... I don't know. This is a lot ta..."

"Sure. Yeah. Sure. Well, uh, let's just wait until we know more and take it from there. Uhhh, also, we are a little curious... It's not unheard of, obviously, in the States, but, uh, it is a little rare and mostly found among immigrants or visitors from developing countries, so we are somewhat curious, epidemiologically, as to how you came to contract this."

"..."

"That is, how you got this illness. How you came in contact with the bacteria."

"How would *I* know?" the befuddled Ansel snapped.

"Well, what do you do? What's your job, your hobbies? You're, uh, from down south right."

"Utinahica..."

"Is that a town?"

"Yes."

"Uh huh. And what do you do there?"

"Game processin', gun range, taxidermist."

Dr. Nguyen leaned back against the stainless steel counter, raising his eyebrows into a visage of serene revelation, and let out a long, "Ahhhhhhh..."

"What?" Ansel seemed almost angered at Nguyen's

reaction.

"You... stuff animals."

"Mount... Yeah. What?"

"Anything out of the ordinary? Ummm, probably a while ago."

"That's what Alvin asked me..."

"Who?"

"Dr. Pirkle. Asked me the same thing. So... it's *the snake!* It was *that dang snake,* wudn't it!?"

"Well, doubtful from a reptile... and, again, probably be years ago, but I'm wondering. Have you, uhhh, had any dealings with... armadillos?"

Ansel's blood went cold. He groaned out loud but thought to himself, "Not the armadillo. Not *Michael.*"

"So, I take that as a 'yes?'"

"Yes."

"And this was long ago?"

"Not really," Ansel looked up, hopefully. "Six months... 'bout..."

"Hmmm..."

"But he... Mullis... he brung it in year ago January, so that'd be when I first messed with it," he went on, almost to himself.

"Hmmm..." Nguyen repeated. "Well, it's been *known* to develop that quickly. But... ummm, well... Yeah. Okay. Usually it takes a *long* time to manifest. Sometimes decades. But, uh, you've got it so I guess that's it. But, uh, yeah, armadillos can get systemic infections and be carriers, so we do see this from time-to-time."

"An' it ain't the snake?" Ansel pleaded broken-heartedly.

"Doubt it. Afraid not. No."

Ansel felt crushed once more and mostly ignored the details of the rest of the session wherein more cuts were made, sample's taken and Dr Nguyen gave him a subcutaneous injection, told him to return in three days and asked if he would be staying in town or would have to make the long trip downstate and back. Usually, Ansel would drive any distance to get out of a city, but there was nothing for him back in Utinahica. Having a room where he could just relax, and walk around without being run from would be welcome. Even here. He asked if there was a Rodeway Inn nearby. The doctor had no idea but was certain there must be many fine lodging options available with I-85/75 so nearby.

Ansel did find a Rodeway twenty minutes away, but that was fine since he didn't want to be in Midtown anyway and there was a Chik-fil-A close by. Aside from the fact that he wished he

The Work

could call Hazel but couldn't, since she now resided full-time at the camp, and that he couldn't eat Chik-fil-A on Sunday because it was closed, Ansel mostly enjoyed his hermitancy at the Rodeway, but most certainly did not rest assured.

•••

Monday morning Ansel checked out and returned to the clinic.

Dr. Nguyen greeted him and, upon inspecting the inflamed lump where he had received the injection, confirmed, almost too cheerily, that Ansel did have Hansen's.

"Okay! So, Mr. Bragg, we'd, uh, like you to return in about three to four weeks to examine this area again but, uh, for now we're confident that you have a tuberculoid, or what's known as Paucibacillary – or "PB" – leprosy. Which is good! So, uh, we're going to go ahead and get you a prescription to get you on an MDT regimen – that's, uh, 'multi-drug-therapy,' because we're going to have you on two antibiotics. So, mmmm, that'll be, uh, Rifampicin at 600 mg – and, uh, that will only be once a month – and then, uh, Dapsone at 100 mg. Now that will be daily and that will be for six months, at least. So, uh, you may have bloody stools, eyes turn yellow, oh, and, uh, that other one will make your urine turn red or orange or maybe *purple*, so that's fun, but don't worry about that... Anyway it's, uhh, all in the literature. But that's it!"

"*That's all...?*"

"That's it for this. So just take this prescription to the pharmacy downstairs and they can, uh, take care of you on that. And we'll have a clinician go over more of the details on beginning and, uh, using the medicines."

"Uh huh."

"But now, with the, uh, neuropathy thing... There are standard therapies in practice – corticosteroids, surgical nerve decompression... and, of course, uh, there will be some decreased sensation management involved, regardless – but we're *very* excited about the promise of the emerging field of venom therapies: Uh, from hornets, scorpion fish, irukandji jellies... just a whole *ark* of creatures!"

"Uh huh." Ansel had no idea where this was going.

"With neuropathies there have been some recent advances with, uh, in particular, the ophiovenins and we would love it if you would be willing to be involved in a test study, *particularly* as this treatment would be most applicable to the, uh, likely acute granulomatous inflammation we are seeing with you. So... whadd'ya think?"

The Work

"I don't even know what you're sayin'. You want me ta volunteer ta be tested with some kinda medicine what's come from poison bugs or fishes or somethin'?"

"Mmmm… *soorrrt* of. And these are ophiovenins."

"Uh huh."

"Funny, they, uh, used to think that snake bites cured leprosy… Hundreds of years ago… All over the world…"

Ansel's hair began to stand on end.

Nguyen continued, still full of cheer, "Turns out they were sort of right…"

Ansel felt as if he was on the verge of a panic attack.

"So," the doctor went on, "ophiovenins…   … From snakes."

"*Snakes! Oh Hell no!* That ain't right!" Ansel shot back, rising to his feet.

"Nonsense Mr. Bragg… may I call you Ansel? This is a marvelous new world we're seeing. We're on the verge of miracles like never before. Many for complications for which these not only represent better treatments, but, uh, also for many for which there were *no* treatments available at all."

"From snakes!?"

"Mmmm, sure. Just part of Nature, Ansel, one of God's creatures." Ansel didn't see it that way. "And, just to explain, for this particular, uh, situation, well, the venom of some rattlesnakes produces a presynaptic neurotoxic venom component – Mojave type A toxin – whose derivatives have been demonstrated to be therapeutic when injected into the diseased tissue of caged rats..."

"NOOOO*ooooooo!!*"

Ansel began to waver around like a tree in the wind. This was too much. He could not accept this. This was against God and now he would rely on God alone to save him. He directed his waving inertia towards the door and staggered out of the office without a word, stumbled down the stairs and out into the street, peeved and filled with confusion and despondency, shaking and mumbling "shoot *snake poison* from rats inta *me...* not on your sweet heinie... crazy, durn doctors... I outta..."

He stomped down the block towards the parking lot staring at the pavement. He stopped at a corner to look up at traffic and saw a man with a shopping cart and his pants around his ankles "walking" across the street, shifting one fallen pants bound ankle then the other slowly towards him. Ansel couldn't unlock his gaze – was frozen, overpowered by the man's superior will. Hazel had warned him about the city: don't make eye contact. But now it was too late, he was paralyzed, like how he had heard snakes hypnotize birds before striking.

The Work

I done stretch out my hand,
an' no man regarded

"Yeah, Yeah, You knows. Tha's right... You cain't 'scape *me*." The disheveled man barked at Ansel: captured in the searing glare of the approaching menace/prophet. "You knows they's all wrong *alright!* Doctor says I gotta disease. *Gam*-blin'! I don't never gamble. *YOU knows* that! *Nobody* don't never gamble 'cause it all already written. Outcome *IS* – but only *JE*-sus know *WHAT* th'outcome is... I'uz that man what didn't have no boat. Tha's right... I'uz that man what didn't have no boat! I'uz washed out ta sea. Standin' on the roof then *turned* that boat *away*. Thought I know'd th'outcome. Jesus be comin' fuh me... There be three. There be three. *He* say, 'I done called, an' you refused, I done *stretch out* my hand an' *no man* regarded!' Tha's why I's what *you* see now. There be three and the outcome. Th'*OUT*-come! Think *you* know? *Sheee*-it, mother*fucker*, 'less you don't feel. You don't feel, brother. There be three, always is, but two for you an' roll on brother... Tha's what you see. Me. There be two..."

All Ansel could think was, "It's not *my* fault..."

The man unlocked his eyes from Ansel and pushed his cart away, releasing him. Now free, Ansel made it back to the world, back to his truck, back to the road back to Utinahica.

•••

The Work

XV

"*What happened?*"

Before, things were... normal: boring, but they were normal... and boring. Nothing needed to make sense then. It just was. Now everything was inside out: not just *askew*, but like the hide of reality had been peeled off and re-mounted greasy side out. This was worse than a life of meaningless existence in an indifferent universe. That would be welcome. This was *all* meaning – *imponderable* meaning – and *inescapable* involvement with a pissed-off, drunk universe just looking for a knife fight.

And for what? Drunks always take everything the wrong way and want to fight for the wrong reasons. How – why – had he come to be as tormented as Job by God for singing His praises? Diseased, shamefully, *by* His angelic warrior and healer? Salvation found only through Satan, snakes and rats? Good was bad, black was white, up was down. This was a nightmare world out of balance, without logic or reason in which Pine and Pirkle had even switched disciplines, for both to reject and condemn him. Making it most difficult of all to negotiate these waters was that he didn't even know who *he* really was anymore or what his own actions meant or how they had brought about the *re*actions he was enduring. He was fighting for air in a swirling whirlpool of existential crisis as French as those old table bronzes that had started this whole thing.

Now he was going to Springfield for the show. What would happen there? And, when he got back "home" – to what? – What was waiting at the *end* of the road?

He thought this same thought over and over the whole way back: once for every milepost between the Perimeter and Utinahica.

•••

The Work

Ansel returned to the shop unhealed. He began to gather up things for the trip to Springfield and thought of cleaning up. The shop had been essentially untended to since the work was begun. The Thompson boy had barely cleaned one whit in all that time: shavings from form work were all over the floor; chemical cans were left out; the bag and rake from his snake hunt were still where they had been left by the slop sink six months ago; boxes of cartridges for the firing range sat atop the wide-open old bank safe he used as a magazine to securely store them, and the cask of carcass shreds remained marinating in the chemical cocktail that, luckily, prevented them from becoming putrescent.

His hands dug in his pockets in absent-minded frustration, nervously working a clump of paper there. He pulled out the folded piece and opened it up. It was the prescription Dr. Nguyen had written at the clinic. He crumpled it into a hard ball and hurled it across the room.

He didn't have the time or energy to think about any of that nonsense now. He didn't even want *to hear* whatever abuse the blinking light on the answering machine brought. He went to bed early. In the morning he rose before sun up, loaded the truck and set out on the road to the freshly tilled cornfields of Illinois. He would just fill the few extra days before the show opened taking his time getting there – and not being *here*.

•••

The Work

XVI

The evening of the first – the night before the show opened – Ansel parked in front of the Springfield Crowne Plaza Hotel & Convention Center and sauntered as a man at ease into the lobby to check in. Refreshed and somewhat renewed from the drive and from the distance he had put between himself and the town that had rejected him, and by pushing the still active infection in his extremities to the back of his mind, he felt as close to good as he had in weeks. The girl at the reception desk greeted him pleasantly – welcoming even – asked his name and looked up the reservation. She dropped her neck down to scowl quizzically at the screen for what seemed like a long time, said, "excuse me just one moment, sir" and walked back to whisper with a woman in a blazer. The blazered woman glanced at Ansel, nodded to the girl then came over to the desk herself.

"Good evening sir. Would you mind waiting just briefly over there by the door? Someone will be out to speak with you momentarily."

"Somethin' wrong with the reservation? I made all these 'rangements back in November."

"Please sir, over there. It will just be a moment."

"Now what?" he thought. He walked over to the door and paced around on the sidewalk for several minutes when he heard his name called."

He turned around to see a larger, crew cut, man in a black polo shirt with "Crowne Plaza" embroidered on the chest and who had the air of a retired cop.

"Mr. Bragg? Cox Johnson, head of security at the Crowne, and... I'm afraid we have a situation here. We've been informed that there may be a public health risk with your presence, so under the circumstances, and erring on the side of

The Work

caution, *and* with our other guest's well-being in mind, I'm afraid we've had to cancel your reservation."

"Cancel my *reservation*? You can't *do* that."

"Well sir, and I am sorry, but I'm afraid we can. We did attempt to call you and left a message so you wouldn't be bothered with... coming here, but we didn't receive a reply and assumed you knew. If it helps any, I am authorized to refund, in full, all deposits and fees."

"This is... this is so... *un*fair..." He felt more like crying than anger and pleaded pitifully, "I've come *so* far..."

"I am sorry sir," the bulky enforcer, who actually felt no remorse, stated officiously, "but you *must* understand."

"*Informed?* Who would a... Who *could have* 'informed'... ?"

"Again, I am sorry sir," the goon continued as before, "but, as they say, I am not at liberty to discuss that."

"Robert. Bobby! *Dookie!!*" he thought. "Well, what am I s'posed ta do? Where am I s'posed ta stay? I got the convention ta go to... the contest... *the work*."

"Well... Mr. Bragg, and again, I am sorry to inform you, but, as I am also with the convention center here, I must also let you know that you will not be allowed to enter the convention area as well. Again, sorry."

Cox Johnson excused himself for a moment then returned with an envelope, which he passed to Ansel with a Playtex Living Glove, borrowed from the kitchen staff, on his hand. Ansel took it without speaking and slouched back to his truck: his posture beaten into a question mark, punctuating his sentence of torment.

He drove on and on to the first Rodeway Inn he came across where, unaware of the danger he presented, he was allowed to rest. Crossing the inn's parking lot, across the highway from ten miles of sleeping cornfield, Ansel looked up to the night sky and at the weird glowing smudge that had appeared there in the previous weeks, where it hung as if wiped there – smeared; as though God himself had, with His great thumb, attempted to smudge away the heavens' brightest star – and Ansel said,

"That thing. *That* is a goddamn sign."

•••

The Work

a goddamn sign

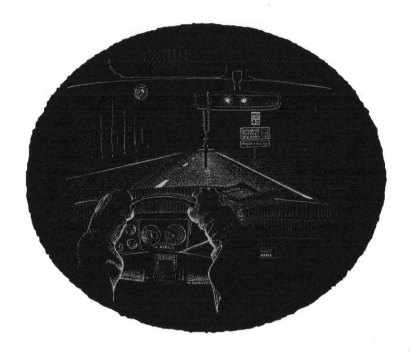

XVII

When Ansel pulled into the gravel drive at the Hide n' Skeet the next night it was impossible not to notice the "PREVERT!" across the entire front of his home as his headlights swept across. It was bright yellow – what appeared to be highway paint.

Highway paint: Robert. Again.

The Work

Ansel drove around to the back, opened the big garage door, backed up the truck and, with almost all of the strength he had left, pulled the work from the truck's tailgate and left it atop the waste barrel. He parked the truck out in the yard and walked back in, looking around. Even with all that had happened he was still bothered by the mess and clutter. He hungered for order. He couldn't let it go any longer and began puttering around doing the cleaning and organizing on which the Thompson boy had dropped the ball.

He opened the old sea-foam green Frigidaire he used for his toxic and flammable chemical cabinet to return the rectangular cans of acetone, perchloroethylene, trichloroethylene, naphthalene… The two, still mostly full, five-gallon buckets of urethane foam mix would not quite fit and were left by the office door so he would remember to deal with them somehow later. He needed to clean the resinous goo from around the spouts and the unsecured lids that, again, the Thompson boy had neglected, anyway.

He picked up the iron rake, the cowbell and the old feed sack from the slop sink. He threw the sack over his shoulder and walked to the other side of the shop to stow the things in the closet. Along the way he stopped to secure the ziggurat of loose cartridge boxes piled upon the old safe. He set the rake down, pulled wide the safe door, and neatly stacked the shells inside with the others.

As he straightened he heard a sound. He walked towards the open garage door at the back of the shop to investigate. Then from behind him, at the front of the Hide n' Skeet, he heard what sounded like a car door slam. He turned again to walk back through the shop when, through the door to the front office, he saw that it was bathed in flickering light. Moving closer, he saw that the light was coming through the window from the yard and panicked.

Ansel ran through the office and out the door to the porch to see a crude cross of scrap wood burning in his yard and Bobby, who quickly, and stupidly, hurled a paint pail of some accelerant at the blaze. There was a brief flash and he bolted through the bucket-strewn lawn, patting out locks of flaming hair as he ran. He got to where two sheet-wearing others were waiting in what Ansel knew to be the Winters' boy's truck, where he turned to yell, *"Nigger lover!"* over his shoulder and leapt into its bed as it peeled away.

Ansel sprinted with building fury across his front lawn and screamed, "*Goddammit Dookie*, least have the *God damned* decency ta wear *the HOOD!!*" at the pickup tearing up the road.

"*Faayggot!*" came back, fading away into the distance.

The Work

Ansel walked back in heretofore-unknown anger and stared at the flaming rood. He tore the feed sack from his shoulder and began to beat violently upon the cross, trying, without success, to put it out. He turned back to the road to scream in anger once more, but, with nothing there at which to scream, he spun back around and, with a real and powerful conniption, kicked one of the paint cans like a place kicker, hard enough to break his toe but, which thanks to his neuropathy, he never knew. The nearly full can bounced off the cross, igniting its contents, and flew to the porch throwing a comet-like trail of flaming petroleum distillate to the front of the Hide n' Skeet, where it then ricocheted in the door and rolled through to the workshop continuing to hurl its blazing cargo like Greek Fire.

The urethane and styrene shavings, invigorated by the fuel, quickly acted as tinder to the rags, the five gallon buckets of bipartite mix, and then to the wooden worktables and finally the building structure. All joined to arouse the fiery furnace seven times hotter than normal. Ansel ran in attempting to discipline these flames with his lash as well, but the fuel the sack had picked up from the cross only seemed to make it worse. With no refractory circle cleared for him by the angels, Ansel could only retreat from the kiln. Staggering backwards in anguish to the yard, he gripped the sack to his head with one hand while shaking the cowbell in randomly metered frustration at his engulfed home and business with the other.

A series of explosions from the back indicated that the refrigerator full of volatile organics had met their flash points, a volley of gunshots followed as the cartridges in the open safe began to fire and, finally, the waste barrel upon which the work sat blew like a cannon, launching the work to tumble end-over-end, trailing a fiery rope of waste solvent and flaming meat scraps, up through the burned away roof into space, then back to the scorched earth where it shattered in a flush of flaming doves and was finally consumed by the conflagration. By then the only thought Ansel could muster was, "I owe Mullis a hundred dollars..."

He lurched back and threw the cowbell at the fire the way an imperiled movie victim throws an empty gun at the fiend bullets failed to stop, then, in utter defeat, dropped to his knees and fell against a big loblolly pine whose rough bark flickered in the firelight. Now and then bundles of needles flashed and sizzled like fuses above him on the branches nearest the flames.

Among all of the chaos and excitement he wondered, "Where are my neighbors – who must see the flames? Where is the fire department? Where is God?" It was as if He wasn't watching the store up there. It was unmanned, abandoned. All

The Work

was still in Heaven.

He began to search his memory of the Bible for some words that might convince the Lord to cease the tribulation He was visiting upon him. Those lovely, poetic and moving portions: the great prayers, the psalms, even the filthy but beautiful Song of Solomon... will they not work? He attempted to compose his own beautiful and eloquent prayer of deliverance: something so heartfelt and moving that it might turn even the scornful heart of the God he had somehow so offended.

His head filled with words.

Nothing but words.

In the end, kneeled and leaning against the solid pine flashing in the dying flames of his life, he hoarsely squeaked, "a gift."

As the flames began to fail Hazel pulled into the drive and around to the back with Norma at the wheel of her truck.

"God damn, Anse! God damn! What *the Hell?*" she yelled from the passenger window.

Ansel Bragg struggled upright on his knees and said, "Dookie..."

"God damn!"

From inside the truck he heard Norma say "Nuh uh!"

"Seen 'im…" Ansel sighed with disdain, then looked up and said, "Where was the fire department?"

"Anse, I *seen 'em*… all… just now up there at the end a the road… up by the County Road, Anse. All parked there, trucks n' ev'rything, just sittin' and a coupla 'em was walked down close in the road – watchin.' Couldn't figure it… It's like they was just standing and waitin'. Like they's seein' maybe nothin' else went up, maybe… or makin' sure the whole place burnt ta the ground. I don't know Anse… But I reckon they ain't comin'."

Ansel groaned, then leaned his head back to the tree and said, "I need somewhere ta go Haze… Somewhere ta *be*…"

"I know Anse. I'm sorry but… Cain't come out to the camp. Not till you're all better…"

"My God, this whole thing… destroyed me. I'm ruined! I'm 'unclean.' *Ever-body* is a liar…"

"I don't know what to tell ya Anse. I really don't – jus' say 'Hell with it all' an' move on…"

"Where *can* I go?" he called back with a mournful resolve. "I don't even have any money…"

"What about th' Chock Full o'Nuts can?"

"Burnt up…"

The Work

"Here, take what I got." She pulled out her backpack and Ansel watched her dig through and pull out everything she had. Behind her in the driver's seat, Norma lit a cigarette. In the lighter's glow he could see the black eye.

He stood to walk over for the money.

"No Anse! Jus' stay there..."

Hazel took all the bills and wadded them up into ball and tried to throw it to him, but the wad broke up like a meteor with its meteorite bills traveling only a few feet and scattered around.

"I gotta go Anse. Norma's talkin' 'bout bein' downwind. I love ya babe. I do. Keep in touch."

Norma put it in gear, scattered gravel around and was off up the road.

Ansel wandered over to where the crumpled bills lay around like dandelion puffs in the grass and began to harvest them. He stooped to pick one and noticed it was different: just white paper. He uncrumpled it and saw it was the prescription from the clinic. Somehow, some vortex created by the fire had carried it out of the shop and back into his hands.

Ansel squatted and, for a long while, stared at the scrap he held in both hands at arm's length.

He looked ahead. Then up. Through the trees and a hole

in the gathering clouds he again saw the hazy glowing smudge on the night sky – the sign. It was bright.

He looked back at the scrap.

Suddenly, *everything* became *crystal* clear.

He was overcome with a calm and peace he understood he had never known. As if he had been dipped in pure waters, all the pain washed away. In a revelation, he knew now, to the deepest core of his being, that God was not just greater than anything, but that nothing greater could even be *thought* and, even within his darkest doubt, it was his own faith seeking understanding that had led him here.

There was *always* hope.

The armadillo *was* a message of Hope after all, and even he himself had not recognized it fully. "There *is* always Hope." Those were his own oft-repeated words. "There *is* always Hope." That was the message he himself had delivered via the armadillo a hundred times. And now here in his own – admittedly, kind of over-the-top – trials, he had despaired and buckled. But there *is* always Hope. And now it all made sense.

There were so many questions at the beginning. Now he saw only answers.

*Every*thing *everyone* had said, *taken together*, was right. They most assuredly did not know it – each piece on its own was

The Work

just a meaningless fragment …no man regarded, but all together they solved the puzzle and formed a picture. Pirkle. Pine, the gospel song, NASCAR, the fat kid with the wires in his tooth… *Dookie*: it *was* that old joke about the flood, and God and the boat, but so much more – even the pant-less, home-less prophet was right, perhaps most knowingly of all.

And, yes, even Ansel himself was right in thoughts he had feared were madness.

It did now come a shower of rain and it was cool and trickled over his skin and carried away the ashes.

His knowledge of the Good Book returned and he sang out,

"For lo, the winter is past; the rain is over and gone; the flowers appear on the earth; the time of the singing of birds is come, and the voice of the turtledove is heard IN-OUR-LAANNND!!!"

The picture formed more fully second-by-second and he felt his strength, and his Faith, return to the point it seemed he had never had any before this moment, and that thought returned anon each following moment as it eclipsed the one that had come before.

"It is never too late. Tomorrow will be better."

Ansel went back to his feet.

"The Lord does plant peculiar seed, don' 'e?"

He looked overhead and all around. In the distance, gentle thunder from the approaching spring storm rolled and faded away. Even the sweet, aromatic funk of his charred and hissing home was ecstasy: renewal. Rebirth. Heaven anew.

Pine cones.

Overcome in the moment of perfect bliss, he placed his hands on his hips, drew a deep breath and grinned, almost giddy, then rolled his head back up to the rain and laughed like a pirate.

Inside the smoldering pile, a few red embers continued to heat the debris.

Three more cartridges went off in the ruins.

Ansel heard two.

•••

The Work

his charred and hissing home was ecstacy

JD Hollingsworth

Afterward From The Publisher

Georgia native JD Hollingsworth writes from his Brooklyn home from where he's produced his first books under Casa Forte Press.

Only a writer with such a wealth of skills, life experiences, and writing instinct could flush out such original prose which Casa Forte Press is honored to represent.

Armed with a rich arsenal of words, from the vernacular to the Latin nomenclature of biological taxonomy, popular history and culture, Hollingsworth's writing delivers a gripping and enthralling universe filled with mysticism, where the reader is transported to the overlooked towns off I-85 South, and where its inhabitants come alive through faithful portraits, in the deep dialect and style of the Southern Gothic.

- Helena Cavendish de Moura